BETWEEN INK AND SHADOWS

MELISSA WRIGHT

BETWEEN
INK
AND
SHADOWS

CHAPTER 1

Nimona Weston was about to do something dangerously foolish. It would not have been the first foolish thing she'd done but possibly the most dangerous. A debt to the Trust had her tied to bargains and theft, to society's sordid underbelly.

She had been born into it, but it was not where she would die. She would regain her freedom, even if she had to resort to underhanded tactics to get it. The Trust would not own her any longer.

She locked the bedroom door behind her then walked barefoot across a rug-scattered floor to her wardrobe. Lace and beads stared back at her, but beyond them, well hidden from common view, waited slim black pants, a trim, long-tailed jacket, and tall boots. In short order, the day's gown was draped over her chaise, and Nim was dressed in clothes that would never be accepted among respectable company. She closed the wardrobe door then took a long draw from the decanter on her desk. As the liquid burned through her lingering dread, Nim slid the hidden panel beside her bookshelf aside to stare into the darkness of a narrow corridor that would give her passage to the streets of Inara.

It was the turn of the moon and time to pay the tithes.

❦

THE BACK STREETS of Inara were shadowed and damp, but the air was warm enough to remind Nim that the seasons were changing again. Springtide was well and truly gone, and she'd been forced to break, time and again, the promise she'd made herself. Promises broken were what she'd come to expect, along with more than her share of unfortunate luck, but it would be different this time. She had no other choice.

Her boot splashed into a puddle, and Nim glanced over her shoulder to be certain she was still alone. A few figures shifted among the shadows, men about the evening's work who paid no mind to the dark-cloaked figure heading to a part of the city best left unnoticed. Kings had their crowns, but the Trust held the power. It didn't matter how one was entangled with the Trust, whether it was the threat of debt, shame, or fear of retribution— to be among court society meant that one could never associate with those who dealt in magical favors.

Her father had taught her that. He'd been highest among them, close to the king. And somehow, he'd gotten tangled in a dark bargain that had cost him his station and his freedom.

He'd been fortunate, though, because others had faced far worse. Nim could recall half a dozen members of court who'd been hanged for the mere rumor of magical favors. The Trust might have held the power, but the king still held the city. Magic was forbidden by law, and far behind Nim, between her evening's destination and Inara Castle, a platform waited on the square for hanging day.

A clatter echoed from a nearby alleyway, and Nim sped her steps. Her gloves felt too tight, her cloak too restrictive. She hated tithe day more than anything, and her list of hates was amply long.

A pair of torches lit the tall arch, its iron gates raised, that led to the undercity. The sentries posted at the entrance were the same as they had been the last ten moons, but Nim did not give sign of recognition when the torchlight flickered over their features. She never looked a member of the Trust in the eyes if she could help it. Contract or no, she would give nothing to the Trust that resembled courtesy. Not after what they had taken from her.

The torches smelled of magic but burned as hot and unsteadily as any that lined the walls of the city's taverns and inns. A bit uninspired when one had access to untold power and yet not unwelcome—the strangest magics made Nim uneasy. It was unsettling to see forces work against nature, to feel their pulses beat with her own. She much preferred those that felt more real, those that could be pretended away.

"Daughter of Bancroft Weston." The voice came from the end of the corridor, from a figure made faceless by the shadows of stone.

"Lady Weston," Nimona said. "I am not owned by my father."

The figure did not move into the sparse light, but Nim could feel his smile. She might not have been owned by her father, but she was owned by his debt. Her life was signed to the Trust.

Nim shoved the hood of her cloak back and gave the darkness a stern look. Losing her standing in society had done nothing to steal the temperament she'd earned with it.

The man let out a breath that might have been a laugh.

She opened her mouth to tell him exactly what she thought of his loyalties, but the door beyond him opened, bathing the corridor in light. She stepped back, even though the woman rushing through paid no mind to either Nim or the sentry. The woman bore a fresh scar from her brow to her chin, the mark jagged, pink, and stark. Nim swallowed any words she might have said. The Trust did not take what had not been bought by them. If the woman was marked, it was because her debt had not been paid, because the beauty she'd bartered for was theirs to reclaim.

The sentry gave Nim a smirk, and she felt the color drain

from her face. Nim was beautiful, too, and a part of her had long suspected that her own beauty had been bought. Those who dealt with the Trust were unable to contain a desire for the things they could not reach on their own. Their debts were often a myriad of small favors, none of which would serve them well at all. Her father had been a bettor, like so many others who sold their freedom for magic, on risks that might someday land him reward. Nim would never be able to answer her doubts until she paid his debt and held his contract in her hands. If he was the reason she was beautiful, he was also the reason his debts had transferred that contract to her.

It was something she'd pondered since she was a girl and her features had started to gain notice. He could have wagered so many things—there was no way not to wonder whether he'd bet on her looks in order to get her a match with someone at court. And to wonder if that bargain had been paid by someone else, if it had been what had cost him Nim's mother—why she'd caught the illness that had eventually killed her—or why Nim had never had any sisters. If those things were true, she might never know what it had cost her father, but it had all been for naught. He was imprisoned in the undercity, and she'd been forced to take on his debt. Whatever he'd owed, it was hers to repay, even if her face would be cut, even if she was to be marked as owned.

The sentry gestured Nim into the room. She drew a steadying breath, wishing she'd taken a second pull from her decanter.

"Ah, ah." The sentry stopped her with a hand on her sternum, and she froze, shooting him a glare she knew she might come to regret. "Weapons," he said.

Nim frowned but was grateful he'd reminded her before she was caught inside with one on her person. She'd been punished before, and it was not an experience she was eager to revisit. She dropped her dagger and small mace onto the stone and waited for him to remove his hand. He did not look at her once his task was complete, and she strode into the chamber beyond.

. . .

NIM WALKED into the space with careful, steady steps, head high, eyes forward, and hands clasped loosely behind her back, the way she'd been taught. Lessons from the Trust were not easy things—nothing was spelled out but could only be guessed by missteps, and one learned quickly. Mistakes cost those who were owned more than just the debt. Foolish errors were paid for with pain.

"Miss Weston." The words echoed through the open chamber, the room's warm glow entirely at odds with everything it represented.

"Calum," Nim replied. It was all she offered. It was best not to speak, even when one thought they had something that needed saying. It was never worth it.

Nim kept her gaze on Calum's chair, though he was not in it just yet. It made the task considerably easier, but her eyes wanted to roam the contracts splayed over his desk. They stank of magic, sulfur, blood, and—somehow—regret. She was aware that somewhere among the untold number of contracts hidden throughout the Trust, her own contract waited. She could not break it, could not remove the seal to even see what was written inside, and no part of her wanted to try even to touch it so that Calum might discover she'd tried and deem her in default of the terms.

"What brings you to my post this evening, Nimona of Inara?" His voice held a purr—evidently, he was in a particular sort of mood. It was not the sort of mood Nimona cared for, though none of them really were.

"Tithe day," she said.

Calum's footsteps were silent, but she could feel him moving closer, feel the heat of his magic ebb and flow against icy waves of fear. An instinct in her said *run*, and Nimona had come to understand exactly how correct it had been. But she was tied to the Trust, and with the contract—so like those spread on the desk before her—she was tied to him, her warden, as well. No matter how preferable leaving might have been, Nim could do nothing but stay.

No one knew where the magic came from. It was older than the foundations of Inara and just as unshakable. The only thing certain was that magic was in the blood. Only those who held it —those of the Trust—passed it to their children. Calum was from the most powerful lineage of all. And Nim was only human.

"Hmm," he rumbled. "You've not much to say tonight." He slid into her view, his dark eyes smiling and his mouth tipped up at the corner. Nim never had much to say if she could help it, especially not when he was so close. Her fingers twitched, but she had to hold them fast and force her gaze away from his.

Calum bit his lip, the point of his incisor somehow predatory even in that brief glimpse. "Do tell me what you've brought, Nimona." His tone felt teasing, as if it said she was his favorite, as if he looked forward to the nights she was forced to come more than anything else. But his long fingers rested on the carved grip of a cane, and those whispered he wanted to strike her with it and make her blood run over the stones beneath their feet. Perhaps both were true.

Nim pressed her tongue to the roof of her mouth and held her jaw still. Her chest was rising and falling steadily enough, but only after years of practice. She released her hands from their grip behind her back, slowly reaching into her vest to withdraw a fabric pouch. She much preferred setting her tithes on his desk, but Calum was standing between her and any flat surface, his gaze devouring her every move. He was maybe five and thirty and looked nothing like the monster he truly was. Had she been a normal lady and he a gentleman of court, he might have been just what she enjoyed. As it was, Calum's grace and well-defined jaw only made her loathe him more. She loosened the string ties and waited for Calum to reach for his due. It was a moment before he finally did, and her chest eased as she upended the pouch over his open palm.

"As you requested." The pendant had been from a lady whose contract was up, and Nim suspected Calum was only toying with the woman before he sent his men. He had no real need of Nim with a hundred merciless accountants at his beck and call. Nim had seen what they could do. She'd felt the magic tear through its victims, the torment it wrought far worse than pain or death.

Calum rolled the pendant between his fingers then slid it into the pocket of his coat. He tugged his hem, not that it needed straightening, but more, Nim thought, in an attempt to draw her eyes.

It didn't work. "Next month's tithe." The words came out as more of a demand than she intended.

Calum wet his lips. "So eager, my lady. We both know there is no reason to rush."

Nim's teeth pressed together hard. What they both knew was that debt was swallowing her, that the interest on her father's contract and the tasks set upon her would not allow her ever to get free. That didn't mean she relished being in Calum's company. The rush was that she wanted nothing more than to escape it. She silently stared at the wall past him.

He let out a small laugh then turned to stroll to the opposite side of the desk. His boots were trim and polished, his uniform impeccable, but Calum's hair was missing a small chunk near the base of his neck. He turned to settle into his chair, and Nim snapped her gaze forward once more. Looking at him had been a mistake that she hoped he hadn't caught. *Don't think of her*, Nim warned herself. Not Calum's mother and head of the Trust. She was too near the woman's lair.

Calum cleared his throat as if he could somehow sense the direction of Nim's thoughts, and she was once again reminded that soon, the head of the Trust would not be a woman they both feared. The head of the Trust would be Calum.

She was grateful for the tonic she'd swigged in her room.

He slid a strip of parchment across the desk. Nim stepped

forward, her gaze only passing over the note, though her hands longed to reach out and touch the fine material.

Then her eyes shot to Calum's. Her heart struggled for rhythm, but she could not say whether it was owing merely to fear. She'd caught his gaze, and he had been ready for it, and Nim could do nothing about it. She was trapped. Worse were the words on the parchment, the task he'd set. *Are you trying to get me hanged?* she wanted to scream, and she might have, had her voice not been snared with her heart in her throat.

Calum's dark eyes seemed to read her mind, his lips curling into a wicked smile. "Yes," he told her. "I do think you'll enjoy this task, won't you, Nim?"

The familiar use of her name snapped her out of his magic's hold on her, and she forced her eyes back to the paper—to the slanted script that read not just the name of a mark but a mark who was the king's seneschal, *Warrick Spenser.*

"It's impossible," she whispered. "How"—Nim swallowed. She would have to gain access to the man's personal rooms, to a suite inside the castle. She could not understand what madness Calum was playing at. The seneschal was second to the king, the very man responsible for the hanging of those who associated with magic, the head of law and order for Inara. "And if I cannot?"

Calum's soft chuckle nearly brought her gaze to his again, where it might have been snared, but the coldness that swept through her stayed her will. Nim was aware of the terms of the tithes, even if she'd never read the contract that bound her to them. To miss her dues would be the end of what little freedom she knew and the death of hope. Calum's tone only confirmed it. "Ask me in a month and see."

CHAPTER 2

Nim was plagued by nightmares worse than the usual tithe-night sort, woke late the next day rumpled and ill mannered, and could not be consoled by rashers or biscuits. In fact, her mood wasn't resolved even after Allister attempted to intrigue her with valet tittle-tattle. Honestly, that the man had even spoken the words "tittle-tattle" should have been enough.

"I thank you for your valiant efforts, my good man, but I'm afraid I'll need a moment to mourn what's left of my freedom."

Allister didn't ask what she meant. He never did. She wasn't certain whether he thought she was just being dramatic or if he suspected the truth and wanted no part of it. It didn't matter. A valet's honor relied on holding his patron's secrets, and though Allister might occasionally pass on a neighbor's particulars, he would never speak of one from his own house. And he never commented on her speaking to him as if she were the man of that house. He was a valet, after all.

Nim pursed her lips. "I have been given a task far beyond my means, and there is no hope for working it out."

He drew a long-suffering breath. "Shall I proceed to get you drunk, my lady?"

Nim snorted and fell back onto the settee. "Oh, that it would be enough." Tossing a hand over her eyes, she thought possibly she *was* being dramatic, but she was more than a little doomed. Nothing had gone as planned. She was in worse shape than when she'd resolved to break free of her contract. She knew she would be lucky to make it out of the task alive. In four weeks, she had to steal a small drum watch from the seneschal's desk drawer, which was no doubt locked or hidden behind a secret panel in some ridiculous manner, or risk being thrown in a dark cell in the depths of the undercity like her father. Or worse, she might have the price of the task taken from her flesh at the hands of Calum Lucus.

A chill ran over her, and she dropped her arm from her face. "No. Drinking won't fix this. I'm loath to say it, but I must at least make a go of it. Something to avoid the regret of not trying as I waste away in the depths of despair." She was destined to lose what paltry freedom she had left with Calum's task—she would either be hanged or miss her tithe and break the terms of their agreement. There was little risk in grasping at straws. Maybe she would end up in the dungeons of King Stewart's castle instead, which was a far improved prospect, should she manage to stay imprisoned instead of being burned or hanged for the crime. She wondered if it was treason to steal from a king's man. A glance at Allister, and she decided it best not to ask. "Please send a note to Margery that I should like to meet her tomorrow afternoon."

He inclined his head. "Of course, my lady. At once."

Nim picked up a biscuit and slathered it with preserves. "I'll miss you, my friend," she whispered to the food as she shoved it into her mouth.

Allister cleared his throat, and Nim glanced up, her words thick around a mouthful of bread. "I thought you left."

His lips tightened in the effort not to laugh at her, but he managed to restrain himself. One of his dark brows lifted, and his gaze fell to the rumpled wardrobe on the floor.

"Right," she said, swallowing roughly as she brushed her palms over her skirt. "Hide the evidence. Good man."

Allister inclined his head, and she was fairly certain he did smile then, but he was gone in a moment, so she bent to pick up her nighttime illicit-venturing clothes. She shook them out, hating the realization that she would be wearing them again in a matter of days—as a thief inside the king's castle. "Cursed Calum," she muttered then glanced over her shoulder as if the name might inadvertently call him.

Satisfied it had not, she stashed her wardrobe away then crossed to the desk. She usually wrote in the sitting room, where the light was better, but Nim had to face getting her affairs in order and had no interest in penning the instructions where the head of the household might happen upon her. She could trust Allister, and only Allister, with her instructions. She prayed that by some twist of fate, he would not need them, but the truth hammered against her in waves of dread and hopelessness. The chance of her succeeding was little to none. There was no way to escape. Should she attempt to flee the kingdom before the contract was resolved, the magic would find her. Worse, breaking the terms would put her in Trust hands that much faster.

The day had started what was likely Nim's last month with any taste of freedom. In a matter of time, she would be hanged or found forfeit in her contract and at the mercy of Calum's monstrous whims.

By THE NEXT AFTERNOON, her outlook had not improved, but she at least made a plan. The list of tasks to order her affairs had been safely hidden where Allister would find them, should she be caught, and she had made the walk to the massive manor that was Margery's family home. Margery's father had long since gone, and her brother was off to fight in the king's army, so Margery and a distant cousin haunted the halls of the manor as if it was their own.

As Nim approached the main entrance, she glanced across the courtyard, a habit she supposed seemed casual curiosity to anyone who did not live in fear of the Trust. She had gotten used to seeing nothing, though, so when a cloaked figure shifted in the shadows of a column, a chill ran over Nim's spine. Her palm found the handle of her dagger beneath her cloak, and she made the decision to turn away from the house. She should never have come to Margery. It was too big a risk.

The door behind Nim opened, and someone snagged her by the cloak. "Nimona."

Margery jerked Nim through the massive oaken doorway. The woman had opened the door herself despite having a half dozen in-house staff, and she immediately clasped their fingers together to drag Nim toward the sitting room. "I haven't seen you in weeks. You're a poor companion, Miss Weston."

Nim managed a smile. She could not warn Margery. There was no speaking of the Trust without putting her friend in even more danger than she'd already caused. She could only hope the figure she'd seen outside was meant as a threat toward Nim. She squeezed Margery's hand. "I'll remind you that the last time I was here, I was chided for trespassing on your time when you had lawyering to do."

Margery sniffed. "I doubt that. 'Trespassing' doesn't sound like a word I would throw around casually." She gave Nim a laughing glance, as they both knew "lawyering" was the word she'd not thrown around. Nim felt a sharp stab of guilt that she might have brought the Trust's attention to her, but Margery was the only one she could come to and the only one who might have the information she needed, even if Margery's work mostly dealt in the crafting of marriage contracts and property transfers.

The women passed into the sitting room, its chaotic arrange-ment bright with the sunlight coming through a row of windows on the far wall. Margery called for tea and asked, "For the love of all things sacred, could guests finally be served some decent cake?" as she led Nim to a set of chairs near the far corner.

"Have you been painting?" Nim asked.

Margery rolled her eyes at the stack of splattered canvases. "Beasley. He's got it in his head he's going to paint for the king someday, the floppy-headed slack."

"That's treason." Nim's whisper was scandalized, though it was clear Margery had been speaking of her cousin, he of the waffling ambition, and not the king.

Margery's brow lifted in challenge, as if she had somehow anticipated treason would be the subject of the day's meeting. She didn't know the half of it. Her braided hair was tied into a loose bunch, the dark brown tinted with dye that warmed to red in the afternoon sun. Most women of society avoided any sort of artificial beauty, given that being accused of buying it through magical favors meant being burned or hanged. But Margery seemed to dare them to make such an accusation, and Nim loved her all the more for it. Her friend had rich brown eyes, a smattering of freckles, full lips, and was tall and strong but oddly terrible at running.

"I've missed you," Nim said.

The playfulness fell from Margery's expression. "Oh, no. I knew an urgent message from Allister wasn't a good sign, but I hadn't expected it would be this bad. What is it, Nim?"

She laughed helplessly. "I hardly know."

There was a light knock at the door, and a slender maid brought in a tray of tea and cakes. She eyed Margery carefully as she crossed the room then settled the tray on a low table near Nim.

"For the sake of—please stop being so jumpy in front of guests. She'll think I've abused you in some horrible manner."

The girl gave her an accusatory glance, and Margery huffed. "Fine. Last evening's cakes were entirely acceptable. It was only that I was in the mood for lemon. Are you satisfied?"

The girl's narrow chin rose before she gave a brief nod of acquiescence then turned to leave the room. Nim's lips turned up at the corner as she took a gingerbread piece from the dish of tarts and custards. "I much prefer her to the last one. She has pluck."

Margery gave Nim a narrow look. "We don't speak the last one's name in this house." She made the sign to ward off curses then winked. "Now, tell me what I can do for you, my dear."

Etiquette might have had Nim inquiring about any number of less dire things first, but she'd been friends with Margery for as long as she could remember, and Nim knew better than to make her wait. "I need information."

Margery shrugged one shoulder. The request was nothing new, and besides, Nim knew Margery trusted her with any bit of information she came across. It was easy enough, given that Nim had no one to repeat the information to—Margery was the only member of court willing to risk association with someone tossed from good society.

Nim had led Margery to believe the information was used in business dealings, and though Margery understood the dealings were private, she'd no idea that it was because they were at the behest of the worst sort of bad society.

Nim's fingers ran across a pleat in her skirt. She glanced at the doorway.

"You're safe," Margery told her. "No one can hear you, and they'd be fools to pass on a word either of us says."

"It's... more complicated than usual." It was evident Margery's patience was wearing thin, so Nim pushed forward. "There could be more than a bit of risk for you, and I want you to understand, truly, that I'll not hold it against you if you prefer to pretend I never asked."

Margery's brows drew together. "Curses, girl, what sort of plot have you gotten into now?"

"What do you know of the seneschal?"

The teacup tottered in Margery's hand, and some of the liquid sloshed onto the deep red of her gown. "The..."

Nim nodded, leaning forward to blot the dampness from her friend's skirt.

Margery snatched the napkin from Nim's hand and clasped her fingers as their gazes locked. "Are you in over your head?"

"Yes. But there's no need to drag yourself down with me—"

"Hush," Margery snapped. "I'll give you everything I know. More, if you need it. That's my promise."

Nim squeezed her fingers tighter. "I don't deserve you."

"No one does, love. It's why I'm alone at five and twenty."

Nim's startled laugh came out in a rush of breath, and she had to push back the emotion she felt welling in her chest. Margery hated that sort of nonsense. "Five and twenty?" Her tone was coy, but surely, they both felt the tension beneath it.

"Five. And. Twenty," she repeated. She set her teacup on the table, brushing her palms together as if doing away with all the rest. "Now, let us delve into the depths of the king's venerable seneschal."

CHAPTER 3

Margery had told Nim what she knew of the king's household, the castle layout, and the habits of the seneschal of Inara and had promised to send over what other information she could find. And Nim, alone at her favorite writing desk, was about to do something more dangerous and foolish than she'd ever planned.

Nim's father had fallen behind on his payments when she was only a girl. It hadn't been long after when Nim's freedom had been taken in exchange for his life. A poor bargain, because he'd had no life at all. She'd been young and foolish—she surely would have agreed—but she'd not been given the chance. Calum had stolen her blood, touched her flesh to parchment, and bound her without consent. That was all it took to steal someone's freedom: fresh blood, clever terms, and the magic of the Trust.

Calum had been younger then but just as vile. And the bindings tied her stronger than most because she had been touched by the magic of her father's bargain—one made directly with the head of the Trust, a dark queen whose power was unfathomable.

Nim's father had been trapped in the dark cells deep in the undercity, beneath the weight of a magic that had slowly devoured all that he was, a sacrifice like so many others who'd fed the magic of the Trust.

Nim would not let the same happen to her.

She tapped her quill into the ink pot, resigned to the words. The decision had been made, and there was no going back on it.

She would never be free until the debt was paid, regardless of whose bargain it was. There was no way to reclaim her freedom from the Trust on her own. She needed help. She needed leverage.

People like Nim weren't embraced by the king's court, but that didn't mean she had to ask for favor. If only she could manage to hold something the seneschal wanted, she might be able to bring him to her aid. There was the certain risk of being hanged, but Nim had never feared the king's men as much as the contract on her life—as much as Calum.

Despite the substance of the letter amounting to extortion, she finished with a polite "I look forward to our meeting" then rested the quill back in its place, folded the paper, and sealed it with wax. "Sealing my fate," she muttered, glancing up just in time to see Allister come in.

He inclined his head, and she gestured toward the waiting pile of correspondence near the edge of the desk. "Have these delivered by this afternoon. Tell the staff I plan to take dinner in my rooms. I'll not be disturbed this evening."

Allister nodded, his dark eyes on her but his manners and uniform entirely in order. "Anything else, your ladyship?"

Nim's gaze drifted in the direction of the high vaulted ceiling. "Nothing that can be helped by you, I'm afraid." She pushed to standing, straightening her skirt before meeting the valet's gaze. "Thank you, Allister. I'll check in with you tomorrow."

He dipped his head at the dismissal and spun, silently disappearing from view. Nim knew he could be relied upon. There were two people in the world Nim trusted, and Allister was one of them—he would see the missives delivered and ensure her evening ventures would not be found out.

She made her way through the long corridor to her suite of rooms in a house that was not hers—an owned woman could possess no real property—but indeed was no less free for her use while its proprietor was enjoying an extended visit to the countryside, one from which he might never return.

"Miss Weston." Elena's greeting was formal and brisk as they passed in the corridor. The woman had been head of household since before its owner had disappeared from the premises, but she did not seem to mind his absence. Lady Weston, it seemed, was of no bother to her, either. As long as she kept her friendship with a member of the house staff and her unseemly undertakings from the woman's notice, all would remain well.

Nim inclined her head politely and carried on, the pad of her shoes silent as Elena's echoed off the walls in their wake. Three corridors and a long flight of wide marble stairs later, Nim glanced over her shoulder as she neared the door to her suite. She did not feel unsafe there, but it felt as if the Trust was always watching and had a hand in every move she made. She pulled the key to her rooms from her pocket and slid the metal into the lock. The latch clicked, and when she opened the door, she was not surprised to find that Allister had already prepared a fire and lit the candles near her vanity. Nim let her gaze trail over the space, but nothing seemed amiss. She tucked her key away and dipped her hands in the basin to wash. By the time she had patted them dry, a knock on the door signaled her dinner being delivered.

"Come in," she told the door. Elena's turnover for maids and servers had been impressive, but the new girl had managed to stay on for nearly a week. Her hands trembled as she set the tray on a low table. Nim asked, "What's your name?"

The girl flinched but turned to curtsy. "Alice, your ladyship."

"Alice," Nim repeated.

The girl looked up, her eyes wide and green.

"You seem you've maybe a chance here, so I'd like to discuss the rules. When my doors are locked, you do not enter. Should the manager of the household inquire whether these rooms have been serviced, tell her yes." Her color rose, and Nim added, "Should the task be brought to question, I will assure her of your faithfulness to duty." Nim clasped her hands in front of her waist and stepped nearer, dropping her tone. "I cannot pay you in coin or jewels, as Elena will search your person, but for your risk, you are welcome to half my rations and may come to me if you are ever in need of a favor."

"My lady..." The words fell out of the girl in a breath, and apparently, whatever follow-up declarations she might have made could not find their way to her.

Nim reached up to tuck a rumpled fold of the girl's uniform into place. "The last half dozen in your position were tossed for being slow. Best make haste."

Alice's attention seemed to snap back, and she bobbed another curtsy. "Thank you, my lady." She was out the door in a moment, glancing back only once with what Nim thought was a desire to verify that she was not falling into some sort of complicated trickery.

Nim had only lied about a few of the girls. At least three had been replaced for being too slow. The others, though, had asked questions they should not have or spoken out of turn. If there was anything Elena couldn't tolerate, it was being talked of among society. Nothing had made keeping Nim's own secrets easier.

She smashed together a hunk of bread and meat from the platter while she unlaced her gown and fussed with the tiny buttons along her sleeve. She could barely stomach food on nights she had to venture to the undercity, but years of experience had taught her it was better to have something other than hollowness in her belly when she was scouting a mark. The king's seneschal was no usual mark, though, and the food felt like sand in her mouth. She tossed it aside after only a few bites then moved the tray outside her door with well more than half the food remaining for her bargain with Alice.

She crossed to her wardrobe, prepared to dress not for bed but for the warm night air. Soon, she would be on the dark streets outside Inara Castle, silent and stalking, ready to plot her way inside.

CHAPTER 4

The following day, Margery sent over several sealed maps and documents she'd been able to secure. It was more than Nim could have hoped for but still far less than she would have liked. Few could be trusted in a task tied to treason, and there was little information to be found on such a private, powerful mark.

"Mark," she muttered, disgusted that she even sounded like the criminal she'd become. Best to get her story straight, though. Should she be caught, nothing she said was likely to save her from the dungeons.

"Except a hanging rope," Margery had said.

Indeed. So it was the gallows or the Trust. She could not flee without being caught, and even the attempt would break the terms of her contract. As it had for her father, breaking those terms meant losing more than just her freedom. Nim had been given his debt, but his future was forfeit. He would forever be owned by the Trust. There would be nothing left of him to restore. It had been too long even before she'd gained his debt.

She stared at her reflection in the looking glass of a bedroom in a home that had never truly been hers, black silk tucked snugly over her pinned tresses, dark cloak over clothes unfit for palace wear. The Trust had gotten her there. The Trust had kept her tied to a life of misery and deceit. She would not let them take what was left—the Trust was not where she would die. Her expression grew grim. "The gallows it is."

She took the hidden corridor from her room to an alleyway outside the manor. Normally, she followed the dark alleys toward the common areas of the city and toward the Trust. But tonight, her steps were swift and sure, despite the objections of her hammering heart, and led her in the opposite direction—toward the stables and servants' quarters of Inara Castle. She'd had a previous task inside those quarters the year before, and though she'd returned the item Calum had requested, Nim was certain the young man she'd procured it from had been killed the following week. There had been a fire and the rumor that as many as two dozen of the castle staff had been lost and not a word of the incident since—not that Nim had been fool enough to ask. Investigation into the Trust was the most expedient way to an unpleasant end. One didn't try to discover the Trust's secrets without coming to regret that they'd even been born.

The layout of the quarters had not changed. The king's men had simply washed the ash from the stone and installed new cots —and new servants—by the following moon. Since taking the throne, King Stewart made occasion to publicly denounce the use of magic, but he did not openly discuss the Trust. Even with evidence that the fire had been their doing, to call them out by name would be akin to an act of war. It was safer to sit in his castle and warn that the use of magic led to such just deserts. It was safer to have anyone who tangled with the Trust hanged before the consequences of their bargains took root.

There were rumors about the king and whispers of how a decade of potential queens had been burned inside their rooms, how dark magic had slithered inside to steal his chance to create an heir.

Nim didn't countenance rumors. The truth, she'd found, was often far worse than any idle gossip would bear.

Nim stepped quietly through the corridors, clinging to the shadows or striding with purpose when necessary, avoiding attention in the ways she'd learned from previous tasks and previous mistakes. Guards passed through the castle grounds on constant rotation. She only needed to appear as if nothing she was doing was out of the ordinary, as if she belonged. Ideally, she wouldn't be seen at all. The change of guards would come in more than an hour, which meant those on duty were wearing down. It wasn't as if the servants' quarters needed a good deal of their attention, in any case. Fire incident aside, no one had much interest in sneaking into a room full of overworked castle staff.

Things became trickier deeper inside the castle, but that too was aided by a previous task. Calum preferred her for tasks near the grounds. She'd been born into a high family and could pass easier than the others—she knew more about how to fit in. She'd once been assigned to procure an item from the mistress of a courtier, and while planning her attempt, Nim had learned the route the woman made each night to enter her lover's chamber.

Nim was not headed for a mere courtier's rooms, though, and no guards had been paid off to keep their silence. So the task was a bit slippery and involved more climbing and hiding than she liked, more risk, and a fair amount of luck. She didn't believe in luck as a rule—Nim's father had carried a coin in his boot for years, and it had done him no good at all—but whatever game the fates were playing, her fortune held.

The lower levels of the castle were grand and imposing, and Nim could not help but feel overwhelmed by their size and ill at ease by the way even the whisper of her cloak echoed off stone walls and high vaulted ceilings. They were nothing compared to the upper levels. The king had posted guards far more frequently, and even the dark alcoves she was forced to hide in were detailed beyond measure. Tiny lions, grand longswords, and bare-bottomed infants curled through carved wood and stone. Every window, every door, every turn of the structure was ornamented. Nim had a thought of Margery's floppy-headed cousin and that maybe he'd been right that he could attain a position in the castle as an artist, but she could not bring herself to imagine him inside such a lavish and dangerous place. Not when even the guards were decorated at every turn, polished steel and sharpened points flashing over finely stitched carved leather.

She took the final corridor with far less speed and estimated that she'd been traversing the route for well more than an hour. The marking of time did not stop. Guards stood at each corridor in the upper level, and Nim found herself settled into small, dark spaces for what seemed like endless delays while she waited for her chance to slip past.

When she finally made her way to the entrance to the seneschal's rooms, the door was locked. Nim drew her most prized possession—her key—from the hidden pocket at her waist then split the thin strips of metal from what appeared to be a skeleton key into what, among other things, was a lock-picking tool. The mechanisms inside the lock were far from silent, but when she pushed open the massive door, its hinges did not scream. She carefully pressed the door closed behind her, putting the lock back in place with a satisfying *click* in a room that was utter darkness.

Beyond black shapes inside the shadows, a thin line of pale light showed Nim another door. She prayed her information was correct, that the room on the other side was the seneschal's private study, and that she was not about to stumble through darkness and into a situation that would have her in irons.

NIM CREPT into a room lit by dim blue moonlight that fell through half a dozen massive arched windows. The centermost frame held her awestruck for a heartbeat, the delicate carvings of its lancet arch so intricate that together they became almost formidable. She shook off the hesitation, unsettled that she could be so drawn to skilled architecture when she'd never been struck by more than passing notice of anything of the sort in the past, and took in the rest of the room.

The far wall held two shelves of bound books, and pedestals stood along the walls and between the windows, displaying sculptures of wood and of stone. A small table stood near Nim, on its surface a tall candle, fine cloth, and a bowl of dark fruit. A chair sat before the table, deceptively utilitarian in shape. Like the rest of the castle, every curve was adorned and ornate. A wide stone fireplace dominated the opposite wall, its hearth cold though the space was warm.

Satisfied she'd found the room that held her intended target and that all was quiet throughout the suite, Nim crossed to the considerable desk near the far wall. It was dark and handsome, simpler than the other furnishings. She traced a finger over its edge, near a plush chair and where the wood was worn from use. The chair, too, held signs of wear, and Nim wondered just how much time the seneschal spent in his private rooms. Surely, Margery's information had been correct, and the king's head of law and order throughout the kingdom truly did spend long days installed in the official workrooms of his post. But there was evidence the desk had been well used. Nim stepped toward the center, between the chair and desk, and noted how the moonlight from the largest window fell perfectly across the writing space.

The surface was neat and orderly, and when she carefully opened the first drawer, the papers inside were as well. She drew out a sheet, and the air rose with a warm, woody scent. Nim glanced over her shoulder, but the room was still, its corners dark where hidden from the moonlight.

The paper was lovely, heavy and thick, its surface smooth. Margery had been right about the seneschal's script. It was strong and elegant and spoke to the confidence a person only gained after writing thousands of pages. It was no secret that Nim had always been impressed by good ink and well-shaped handwriting. Of course a seneschal would have a good hand—he would write logs and letters and laws. "Why should I care about his handwriting?" she'd asked Margery, despite all the rest.

Margery had smirked. "All your favorites write well. It's like you collect them. Your pets."

"Pets," Nim had parroted with a snort. But the mark had hit true. Margery knew things about Nim that no one else had gotten close enough to discover. It was past time to draw away— if she wanted to keep her safe, Nim would leave Margery alone.

She pushed the unpleasant thought down and scanned over the correspondence before returning it to the drawer. On top of the neatly stacked pile, she laid the letter she'd brought with her, a sealed message that demanded a meeting if he wanted to see his precious watch returned—a warning that she knew of his ties to the Trust.

Her last chance to gain freedom was by extorting the hand of the king. It truly was an exceptionally foolhardy plan, but she'd no real options, given that she had a month to return the watch before Calum assigned her a new and potentially more dangerous task. If the seneschal could offer her some sort of protection or aid in an escape, Nim would take it. If not, the watch would be delivered to her warden at the turn of the moon. She stared at the letter for only a moment before sliding the drawer closed.

Nim fished through the other drawers but found nothing aside from pen and ink, a tin of what might have been tobacco, and more papers. She frowned, glancing over the desk's construction. There were no locks to be seen, no obvious place where the structure might be thick enough to hide a compartment. But her instructions had said the portable drum watch would be hidden within the seneschal's private rooms, inside his desk. Nim had never seen a portable watch, but a little research had awarded her a sketch of a round bit of carved metal, small enough to fit in the palm of one's hand. She assumed whatever the Trust was after was hidden inside the drum. Why Calum needed it should have been none of her concern, but she suspected the items were tied to her marks' bargains somehow, owed to the Trust. Once she stole them back, Calum would be free to enact his punishment without fear of losing the bartered item. His accountants were more cruelty and brute force than stealth, and given the way they relied on magic, none of them would be able to sneak into a castle courtyard, let alone the seneschal's rooms, without gaining notice.

She knelt below the desk, feeling its surface for a sign of any hidden latch or grooves. Her fingers crossed over joint work so smooth that it was difficult to be certain. She shrugged off her cloak and slid farther beneath the wood, searching out dark corners and edges but finding nothing.

Nim sighed and slipped from under the desk, standing again to lean over its top. Aside from the edge and the writing area directly in front of the chair, the wood grain showed no wear. None but one odd mark on the front edge of the desk. Nim could imagine a figure leaned against it, his hand resting over the ledge. Leaving her cloak sprawled on the floor, she walked around the desk, tapping a knuckle at intervals on the sides of the wood. It echoed back: *Solid. Solid. Hollow.* A slow grin slid across Nim's lips, and she pressed her fingertips over the hollow area's trim. A small point of the carved embellishment slid down like an opening wing, and beneath it was a thin slip of wood that served as a latch. Nim drew her key from her pocket and slid the metal lockpick through the latch. The panel came free noise-lessly to reveal a narrow coffer.

She wiped her palm over the thigh of her pants and thanked the fates. The entire ordeal was taking longer than she had, and it was past time to steal the fool thing and be gone. She was beginning to hope she might actually get away with it. Nim carried the box to the back of the desk for better light, but when she opened the top, there was nothing inside. She whispered a nasty curse.

"How very vulgar," someone said into her ear. The breath was hot and close, and Nim's heart slammed into her chest. She spun, but the figure was already pressed against her, his grip tight on her wrist. She gasped, suddenly trapped between the desk and a hulking man, and as her back leaned precariously over the wood, Nim stared up at her captor, the man who held her wrist, the seneschal of Inara.

CHAPTER 5

The lord Warrick Spenser stared down at Nimona, his hard features outlined by moonlight and shadow. He hovered unbearably near, his thigh pressed to hers, not allowing a single chance for escape. He did not appear to react in the way she might have suspected from a man in his situation, could she even imagine the proper response at all. Given that he was a king's agent, at the least, she would have expected a call for his guard. But his gaze only narrowed on her as his fingers became a manacle around her wrist. His grasp on the thin bones of her wrist was short of painful but tight enough to make her unable to deny that she could not fight him and win.

Nim was slender but not slight and reasonably tall. She'd never had much trouble handling men—outside the Trust, of course—and the weapons at her side were not merely for show. But the man towering over her radiated strength and confidence. They both knew she didn't stand a chance against him.

He raised his free hand beside her. "Is this what you're after?" His voice was a low rumble, though Nim doubted anyone would hear a word they spoke even if she screamed. Not that she was considering it.

As he held the timepiece in his spare hand, her gaze

remained steady and trying for uninterested, but she knew her pulse ticked beneath his fingertips, her chest rising and falling beneath his in too-quick breaths. She had stolen into his rooms, left a message in his desk. There wasn't exactly a route to talk herself safely out of a mess of such proportions, so Nim held her tongue.

He set the timepiece on the desktop beside her. She held very, very still, every inch aware of the heat of him in the thin space between them and where his legs pressed to hers. The room was dark, lit only by moonlight, and his eyes seemed unnaturally green, his brow drawn low.

"They won't let you go, even if you succeed. But you know that."

Nim startled, her mouth coming open. No one spoke of the Trust. No one dared. And certainly not a king's man.

His gaze roamed over her in what she thought was an attempt to instill fear. The look hadn't worked. His words, however... The man had mentioned the Trust—he knew her secret. He understood she'd been sent on a task and that she was afraid she would never get free.

"And yet," he said, his words rolling over her, "here you are."

She didn't reply, dread a vise around her throat.

The seneschal did not back away from her. "You realize it means death to steal from a king's man. Surely, at the least, you understood there would be extended torture and the possibility of being tossed in the dungeons." His tone turned conversational. "Stewart's favorite dungeon is quite disagreeable."

He watched Nim's throat work then drew his eyes from the movement with a slow smile. "All that risk, knowing full well, should you be caught, the society will not protect you. You'll still owe them, your debt accruing while you're imprisoned, alone in the dark depths of Inara Castle. Or worse." His last words came in a whisper, as if toying with her, dangling her attention on a string. "So why? I ask. What price do you put above your own life by stealing into the heart of a king's house?"

The silence stretched before her word slipped free. "Freedom."

"There is no winning freedom from the Trust." Nim's jaw went tight, and he added, "Not even in death."

He'd hit his mark, but he didn't stop there. "The contract is not yours. You inherited a debt."

Panic welled in Nim—the king's seneschal knew too much, impossibly so—but the man straightened, suddenly giving her room to breathe. It didn't last long.

"You're trapped."

She felt defiance flash in her gaze, and he moved forward again. His free hand gripped her hip as he released her wrist with the other to fish in the pocket at her waist. He retrieved her key. "No," she said. "You can't."

His brow shifted. He already had.

She watched in horror as he tucked it into the waist of his own pants. Nim became aware, quite suddenly, that he was wearing nothing over a thin shirt and pants. It was not particularly commonplace to have a visitor hours before dawn, or, she imagined, he might have dressed for the occasion. She shook off the odd thought. "I need that. You can't take it."

His mouth twisted in wry disapproval. "As you steal from beneath my very nose."

He kept hold of her hip, his thumb pressing a warning, careful and deliberate, his gaze steady on hers. She didn't know what was wrong with her—she was acutely aware that she should not feel herself drawn to a man who might see her hanged. "And so, thief, I give you a choice. Death or a bargain?"

Nim's confusion had to have been plain on her face, but she could not seem to find the ability to form a proper reply. "What?"

"You're already caught. Nothing could incriminate you more. You are in the private rooms of the king's seneschal. There could be no single excuse that might find you a way out. What I'm offering is all there is."

There was something curious in his manner, and her fingers trembled where they pressed onto the desk, holding her tipped backwards as he leaned over her. She had no idea what he wanted and couldn't fathom why he would propose such a ludicrous proposition, but she knew better than to trust anything that might bind her. "I don't make bargains."

He couldn't seem to help the soft laugh that slipped from his lips. "So much honor for a thief."

She glared. An overwhelming desire to lash out at him seared through her, followed by one to run. But he was right. She was trapped. "I'm not a thief." She wasn't up for trade.

The seneschal reached into the drawer beside them and drew out the letter she'd left in his desk. Nim's resolve crumbled. There was no coming back from a written threat.

The letter was addressed to him. With her seal. In her hand.

He cracked the wax seal then flicked open the parchment with one hand.

Nim's eyes closed for a long moment, the words echoing through her mind: *If you want to see your watch again, meet me on the square beneath the banners at midnight.*

"Extortion," he said, making no effort to pin down the beginnings of a smirk. "From a woman who doesn't make bargains." He dropped the letter onto the desk beside the timepiece. "Take the watch. It doesn't matter to me. It won't be enough to draw me out."

Her gaze flicked to the timepiece, but she didn't make a move. It was a trick. It had to have been.

"Do you know why they want something personal?" he asked.

Her eyes came back to his. His jaw was square and shadowed, his mouth a solemn line. She did not know. She *wanted* to know.

"It's how they work the theurgy to draw someone back."

"Back," she heard herself say. "Back to the Trust. You're saying..." She shook her head, shifting as far as she was able from him and from the watch. "If they would use that thing to try to bring you to them, why would you give it to me?" *Why would you give up your freedom?*

He leaned toward her. "Because it won't work. I've never become attached to material things. None of it matters."

She gestured disbelievingly to the room, a space filled with rich treasures, artwork, sculpture, and trinkets from far-off lands.

The seneschal's hand shifted on the desk beside her, trapping her from edging any farther away. "Gifts to a man of the king. All for show." His tone echoed the import: *none of it matters*. "That watch will not give your keeper what he wants. This will not end tonight."

Heat rose to her cheeks, and she turned her face from him. *Her keeper*, he'd said. Because Nim belonged to the Trust.

"He wants you to think you've done this on your own. That you've decided to accept his tasks to buy your freedom. But you suspect, deep down, that there's more," Warrick said.

Her gaze snapped to his.

"He's been training you, I'll wager. Giving you tasks that fit so well with what you needed to reach your mark tonight—such a high and dangerous post surrounded by guard and law." The blood drained from her face. That much, she'd considered, but she certainly hadn't expected to hear it from her mark. "How long?" he asked her. "A year? More? How many incidents in the kingdom were created simply to cover your tracks? Fires, deaths, floods, all to hide any trace of a thief in training. Of a lady meant to spoil the seneschal of Inara."

Nim's stomach dropped. "You're lying," she whispered. Her gaze fell to his waist in an accusation. He'd stolen the key from her and was teasing her with discussion of her keeper, trying to tie her to a bargain when he was the very man who held her trapped. "You'll never let me free."

He straightened. "Lying is for cowards. I have nothing to fear." He let his fingers slide from her waist but gave her no space beyond the sliver of moonlight between them. "You can take nothing from me. Why would I need to lie—to cover anything of myself? I'm bare to you, my lady."

She stared at him, incredulous.

He held his hand wide. "The bargain. I hand you to the king, or you become my agent."

CHAPTER 6

Nim stared at the man, certain she'd lost touch with her senses, as any sort of reasonable existence seemed to have floated well out of reach. "A bargain," she said, apparently out of touch, too, with a word that she'd so often despised. There was a possibility that the whole thing was some elaborate trap, but she could not fathom how or why Calum could have maneuvered an agent of the king to be involved. Nim wasn't important enough to warrant attention from a king, not even for her ties to the Trust. She was trapped, well and truly, but not by the Trust's deceit. She was caught by a man of flesh and bone.

He stood only inches from her, his gaze intense, his presence enormous. He'd snatched her wrist with the speed of a viper, and she could still feel the pressure of it, how easily he could have snapped the fragile bone. But he hadn't. He'd only kept her still. And though he'd released first her wrist and then her hip, he still had her pinned beneath his gaze—beneath the pressure of his threat.

A bargain. The words she'd written in her letter echoed again. She'd been a fool to think that she might persuade him, that she could have outmaneuvered a man of his station with threats and trades. Calum had known she would never retrieve the watch without being caught—and somehow, she'd landed in a mess more tangled, because the seneschal's offer was not the sort of trade that dealt with material things.

If she accepted it, she would again be contracted for her freedom, no longer solely from her bindings to the Trust but from the threat of imprisonment. *Or worse*, the seneschal's words reminded her.

"What are your terms?" Her voice was stronger than she expected, but she felt no pride in it. She'd lost everything. It was only a matter of dealing with consequences.

He crossed his arms. "You do everything I say, and I don't hand you over to the king."

She stared up at him. "Those are entirely appalling terms."

One of his sturdy shoulders lifted in a shrug, and Nim wondered at Margery's description of him being graceful. Beneath dark hair, he was all sharp angles, the lines of his body more power than grace. It was hard not to be entirely aware of him with the man so near. "I don't make bargains," she said again, "and certainly not open-ended ones."

"So you choose the king's punishment." He straightened, adjusting the sleeve of his shirt as if preparing to call for the king, despite there being no cuff or jacket present at his wrist.

Nim pressed her eyes closed for a horrible moment. "Of course I don't choose the king's punishment."

"There is no third choice. It is the king or it is the bargain."

Her anger flared. "Do you always speak with such condescension?"

"Yes. How else is one to know of my superiority?"

Nim gritted her teeth. "Your fancy dress, perhaps. I hear you've jeweled buttons and metal pins to cover your jacket and robes. A silver coronet upon your head."

The corner of his mouth twitched, and he mock-bowed toward her in his flimsy undershirt. It brought him too close.

"How can you expect me to bargain with a stranger?" She

knew practically nothing of him. He could have been worse than Calum. "How could I possibly trust you?"

His expression melted into something entirely solemn, his voice low. "I'm bare to you. I vow to only speak the truth to you."

A strange surety accompanied his words, a sensation that told her as plain as a pikestaff that the seneschal was no mere man. He held power beyond his station—he had magic. *Like the Trust.* Nim's fingers were suddenly scrambling for purchase as she tried to back away from him over the top of the desk. She was half across when her feet, caught in the tangle of her cloak from the floor, resisted her frantic jerk to get away, and she lost her balance and tumbled over the other side. The seneschal did not save her.

Nim landed solidly on the wooden floor with a grunt. The panic had not subsided, but when she shot to her feet, he was still standing opposite her across the desk, his hands folded casually behind his back, his expression grave.

Her finger rose like a dagger to keep him back. "You," she said. "You're one of them." She felt the spike of his surprise wash over her and realized she'd been sensing intimations from him all along. She'd just been too distracted to realize. It was too unreasonable to believe from the man who carried out the law. Not him.

His brow shifted the slightest amount, but his voice was steady and too calm. "How can you be certain of that, my lady?"

She glanced toward the door—locked—then the arched windows and their narrow panes of glass. She knew because she could feel the magic crawling over her like... but no, it was not the same. Another reason she'd not realized. When she sensed intentions from Calum or the sentries, it was as if serpents slithered over her skin. From this man, it was something else, a rising warmth that did nothing to urge her away. And it was the absolute last thing she'd expected.

He was an agent of the king. A mark of the Trust. There was no way it could be possible. And yet it was.

"You can sense it."

Nim felt something strange from him, something that might have been disbelief or distrust, but it was quickly driven into resolve. Whatever he thought of her, however rare it was that she had been touched by magic, that she could feel both the power and intimations, he saw that it was true.

"And because you can, you know well that I speak the truth. You can feel that my vow is yours." He stepped back then settled into his chair. As his gaze met hers again, he said, "That is how you know you can trust me, Nimona Weston. Because my intentions are nothing like theirs."

CHAPTER 7

Nimona's fear was like a knife blade shearing her in half. Not only was he one of *them*, but he knew her name. A curse superior to the one he'd called vulgar slipped from her lips.

The seneschal smirked. "Come now. Don't tell me you aren't familiar with my name as well."

Of course she was, because he was her mark. The thought sent a shiver of unease through her, and all the suppositions her mind had been sorting into answers reshuffled. "You knew I was coming."

He reached for a decanter then poured a finger of amber liquid into a glass. "I did. Though not tonight." He ran a hand over the trim of a small side table, pressing his thumb against the wood to reveal a hidden drawer. Nimona tried not to gape as he drew a letter free, its shade horribly familiar and its vermilion seal cracked. It read the name of a lord in Nim's precise hand, a lord she'd written in her inquiries into the seneschal of Inara. He opened it carefully, as if glancing over the paper to remind himself of her words. "You see"—his eyes met hers—"your letter was intercepted and handed over to me by a trusted agent. And it seemed it was not the only inquiry that was made. I was intrigued that someone of your station seemed so desperate for details of the castle schedule, so I looked into your history."

Ice shot through Nim.

The seneschal, Lord Warrick, took a slow slip from his glass. "There was surprisingly little information available for a lady residing in Hearst Manor, but, as you might imagine, that only intrigued me more."

Nimona did imagine. She imagined he'd heard right away about the gentleman Hearst's unexpected and extended departure from society. She felt the urge to back away again, but there was nothing to edge toward, aside from a sealed window and a locked door. "I didn't kill him," she heard herself say.

Warrick chuckled darkly. "I am glad to hear it." A silence followed, in which Nimona considered whether the man *had* actually been killed. She might not have believed it before, but Warrick's suggestion that the Trust was covering her deeds with fire and flood was worming its way through her recollection of the recent past. The servants' quarters at the castle, the lady's maid near the river... each of those tasks had been followed swiftly and severely by disastrous events. She'd known the Trust was involved but hadn't suspected any of it was to cover her tracks. And yet, every time she'd stolen back an artifact that had belonged to the Trust, her mark had disappeared. There was no way to be certain they were only being held in a cell.

His finger tapped the side of the glass. "I had you followed."

Nim felt her face pale. They would have seen her go to Margery and would have known about the messenger her friend had sent with information on the king. Nim's mouth came open, but the words lodged in her throat.

Warrick's head tilted to the side as he examined her. Her lip quivered, but she bit hard into the inside of her cheek and forced her distress into a locked box deep inside her. Margery had only tried to help. She'd never been involved in the seedy, sordid things Nim had done.

"I'm not—she isn't who you might think she is. She doesn't

know what I—" Nim drew a steadying breath. "She doesn't know about my ties to the Trust." She didn't know that Nim was involved or that her life was bound by contract.

Warrick's tapping finger stilled on the glass. "The lady Margery? You care about her."

Nim couldn't hide it. The emotion had been plain on her face.

The idea did not seem to please the seneschal. "I'll ensure she's protected."

A strange fluttering beat through Nim's chest. He wasn't lying. She could feel the truth from him. Margery would be safe. "I'll do it."

Warrick's distracted gaze snapped back to hers.

"Your dreadful bargain. I'll do it. If you can protect Margery and keep her safe from the Trust, I'll be your spy."

"Agent," he corrected. "And it's hardly dreadful." Nim stared at him, and he added, "given the alternative."

He stood and crossed to her, the long line of his body lit by moonlight that dipped into shadow on his opposite side, splitting him into two. *Graceful* was not the word that came to mind. *Predatory. Wolfish.* Those were the words her friend should have used. Nim wondered what she looked like to him, standing in that same light, torn between her agreement with him and a contract held by the Trust.

Warrick reached out a hand. "So we have an understanding."

Nim's eyes rose to his. She swallowed her first response then placed her palm against his. Something strange swelled through her, a feeling from him that she could not unravel, as his warmth spread through the bare touch of their hands. Her voice was breathy, not her own. "Yes. It's agreed."

His mouth shifted as if it could not decide whether it meant to form a smile or a frown then settled into a stern line. "It's done, then." He withdrew his hand from hers. "I'll send a messenger with instructions."

The abruptness in his change of tone startled Nim from her

shock. "How can I—what madness do you have planned? They obviously watch me. They will know that I'm plotting against them with the king."

"No," he snapped through the quiet room. "You are not plotting with the king. You are plotting with the king's seneschal." He leaned toward her and lowered his voice. "And should you be caught, I will deny any knowledge of you or our agreement."

Nim's mouth fell open. "You vowed not to lie."

"I vowed not to lie *to you*, Miss Weston. I could not very well hold a position in the king's court by never lying at all, let alone keep my head attached to my neck."

An exasperated sound startled out of Nim. "How do you expect to carry on without the king or the Trust discovering us?"

He gave her a look. Nim crossed her arms. He held up the small drum watch, which she'd not even seen him retrieve from the desk. "This," he said. "You had less than a month to secure it from my private rooms. They will assume, should they become aware of our correspondence, that you are earning your way into my suites. And the king..." Warrick shrugged. "It would do my reputation little harm if a lady were seen stealing into my rooms in the dead of night."

She felt her expression sour and made no attempt to hide it. "They will assume nothing of the sort if they've paid a bit of mind to my conduct thus far."

The tilt to his brow seemed to imply he'd just caught her pilfering his desk in a pair of slim pants.

She raised her chin. "May I have your leave to go, your lordship?"

"Warrick," he said. "And yes, it would be a great relief to resume the privacy of my suite."

A great relief. She could not say she disagreed, but she'd never been dismissed quite so bluntly by a man of high station or no—and one who'd vowed never to lie to her, no less, which meant it was nothing but truth. Nim started for the door then turned. "I need my key."

The glance he gave her said that it was hardly a key, and she knew it. She was very much going to dislike having an additional keeper who could intimate so much with a look. "You don't need a key. You can leave through the corridor."

Nim stared at him. "What corridor?"

He gestured over his shoulder, toward a shadowy corner behind the desk. She bit back another curse at the realization that he'd been watching her the entire time. She would think about how she'd shucked her cloak and climbed the furniture later. "The corridor," she echoed. She would not need a key, he'd said. He was showing her a secret passage. His rooms would essentially be unlocked to her.

The seneschal of Inara had opened his suite to her.

"I'll remind you," he said, "that should you be caught, you'll be thrown in the dungeons or hanged, depending on the king's mood." His gaze took on that curious manner again. "But as you seem to enjoy scampering about in the dead of night, you might well be safe."

"I need it for other things," she said. "The key, I mean."

He gave a single, short shake of his head. "You'll not need it while you're working for me. Anything you require will be supplied. Your purchases will be covered by an ample purse, and requests for anything else can be sent through my messenger."

She gaped at him, aware she'd been vacillating between a sagging jaw and clenched teeth for however long she'd been trapped in his acquaintance.

Warrick apparently seemed to think she was a bit witless, as he repeated the terms of their agreement. "You have one month to return the watch. When that happens, they will assign you a new task. In the meantime, you'll only be stealing for me. Any keys you need will be provided."

"I—" She pressed her fingers to the bridge of her nose. "I think it best that I go now." Before she said something she might regret. Before one of them had enough of the other.

Warrick nodded. "There is a light inside near the doorway.

Take the third turn and then the second. Leave the lantern in its alcove near the exit."

She nodded numbly then made her way to the hidden corridor at the edge of the room.

"Nimona."

At the sound of his voice, she glanced over her shoulder. He was watching her, and that strange sensation she could not quite make out washed over her once more. His face was turned toward her, made pale by the moonlight. His eyes seemed to glow in an unsettling shade of green.

"Don't get caught."

CHAPTER 8

Nim walked in a daze through the streets of Inara as the glow of sunrise crept over the city's dark stone walls. She'd come out of a hidden corridor deep within the castle, its entrance entirely disguised by magic that had not been bought by the Trust. Warrick had powers of his own—that much was clear—but his magic felt nothing like the unpleasantness that was Calum's.

The seneschal had offered the bargain because he knew who she was, who she had been, and about her father. Her name was already sullied, and should she be caught, he could deny everything.

She was tied to an agent of the king in a bargain that might see her hanged. The Trust still owned her. Calum was still her keeper. She'd gained nothing but another binding and more tasks.

A bell rang far off in the city, and wooden clatters echoed from the stables outside the inn. Inara was waking, but Nim felt as if she'd fallen into a hideous, unending dream.

By the time she reached the manor, dawn had crawled over the slate roof and into the upper-level windows. Nim took her own hidden passage, well aware that it was no secret to the seneschal and his watchman or to the Trust and theirs. She trod on, arriving in her room to the cold welcome of a dead hearth and unlit candles. Unlacing her boots, Nim realized her cloak remained in the seneschal's room. She grumbled as she climbed onto her bed.

She did not sleep but sat, staring blankly toward the wall of her bedroom in the stolen house of the gentleman Hearst. Hearst, who might have died at the hands of the Trust or might be deep in the dungeons with what was left of the man who had been her father. She did not know which idea was preferable or whether she cared to find out the truth.

The soft click of metal came from the lock on her bedroom door, followed by the whisper of its hinge. Her stolen valet approached the bed. "My lady." Allister's voice was nothing but quiet concern.

She glanced up at him and blinked. "Oh good," she managed. "I'm glad you're back. I've lost my key. I'm afraid I'll not even be able to get in and out of my own rooms." A helpless laugh escaped her.

Allister's brows drew together. "Of course, my lady. I'll have another one made."

He very well knew the key meant more to her than that. If he knew anything at all, Allister knew she was in trouble.

"Perhaps some tea," he offered carefully.

"Did Alice make it?" she asked absently. "I like her."

"Yes." He crossed his wrists loosely before his buttoned jacket, proper posture for a dutiful valet. "I believe she has a chance."

"Good," Nim said, echoing "I like her" before promptly collapsing onto the bed.

NIM WOKE with a start some time later, based on the low sun through her window. The lingering scent of smelling salts hovered around a too-close Allister and a wide-eyed Alice. The girl let out a sigh of relief. Allister looked down at her. "What have we learned today?"

"Don't bury them until you're sure they're dead."

"Very good," Allister said. "Now, fetch hot water, and we'll review proper tonics."

The girl gave no more than a small nod before she darted from the room.

Nim waved a hand and coughed. "For all things sacred, what have you done to the salts?"

"They are certainly stronger," he agreed. "I'll work on it for next time."

Nim groaned. She prayed there would not be a next time, but there was only one alternative to guarantee she would never again be overwhelmed by the presence of so much magic, and being hanged by the king seemed like no fun at all. "Thank you for letting me sleep first."

Allister stepped back. "Not much else could be done about it, to be honest. You resisted my first several attempts at waking you."

"Regardless," she said, "I'm grateful to have the rest."

One of his sharp brows hitched up.

"I'm not saying it has improved my mood or my situation. Only that I needed a clear head."

"Ah." He straightened the hem of his jacket. "Well and good, then. I've just the thing to help with that." He directed her to the chaise, where a full breakfast waited on the table, complete with half a dozen biscuits and a heap of rashers.

Nim stared down at the spread. "Why would you think I would need all this food? Did I seem starved? Have I been out for a week?"

Allister cleared his throat. "It seems the girl Alice has put in a request at the kitchens—or, to be more precise, a complaint that the lady Weston was not being served as well as she might."

Nim glanced at the myriad of plates then back at Allister with a snort of laughter. "I like her."

Allister inclined his head. "As you said, my lady. Repeatedly." His gaze trailed over the table and Nim's tripled rations, even counting that they were to be split into two. "She does have a way of filching one's regard."

Settling onto the chaise, Nim layered a variety of food between two biscuits and pressed the lot together, Allister's disapproving brow be damned. She let out a relieved sigh and crossed her stockinged feet atop a pillow, her eyes on the poorly rendered but impressively tranquil painting above the console table that depicted a dog curled at the foot of its master's bed. At least, she thought it was a dog.

"A clear head," Allister said.

"Indeed. We've doubled our trouble, my good man, and only a solid plan will get us through." The "us" lingered in the still silence for a moment as Nim took another bite of her afternoon breakfast. "I mean *me*, of course, but it feels far more exciting to plot as if we were a cast, don't you agree?"

"Exhilarating," Allister agreed.

"It's all secret, of course. You'll have to leave. A proper shame, too, as I suspect Alice would be quite dashing with a dagger sheath strapped to her thigh."

The girl stood at the doorway, tea tray in hand.

Allister's mouth twitched, but his propriety crumbled no farther. Nim gave him a look meant to imply that she would get to him eventually. He made every indication of not receiving the message.

The two talked through tonics and cures while Nim finished her breakfast, and by the time she was dressed and back in her room, they presented her with the results of their work. Nim took it without hesitation, if only to spare the pair's feelings, and tossed back the warm liquid before her courage fled. "Burns a bit," she wheezed, "but it will do." She gave a satisfied pat to her sternum then a salute at the tonic's providers.

The wide-eyed girl turned to Allister. His nod contained a far more complicated message that Nim guessed was in a language only the house staff possessed in order to convey the ridiculousness of their employers. "Right," Nim said. "Now off with you."

Allister and the girl gave perfunctory bows before fleeing the room. Nim fluffed her skirt then retrieved her worst-case instructions for Allister. Previous plans had gone to cinder and ash, so all that was left was to rewrite her fate.

CHAPTER 9

Nim was in the drawing room when the first letter came. She'd been elbow deep in notes and distracted by a book she'd accidentally come across that listed the penalties for treason and the ways in which especially creative and unpleasant punishments had been carried out by Stewart's forebears. It did not feel like a particularly productive distraction, but she was quite unable to stop herself.

"Lady Nimona Weston," Allister said from the door.

She glanced up at him, likely appearing as preoccupied as she felt.

"A messenger."

Nim blinked at the valet's presentation then noticed that a still figure waited at his back, the boy's fine jacket trimmed in the king's colors, his posture stiff and formal. "It's all right, Allister. Please do let him past. I'm certain it must be urgent for a—" She flattened her palms against her skirt. "Oh, a *king's* messenger." Nim had a feeling that Allister had not fallen for her feigned surprise, but the production had not been for him. "Why, yes," she told the boy as he approached. "Of course there would be no other reason to flaunt protocol, aside from urgent business from the king. I daresay, we must be needed at court straight away for such a—"

"Lord Warrick sends his regards." The boy stopped well in front of her in a swift bow, apparently oblivious to her pronouncements, his hair falling forward and somehow reminiscent of a chicken on the loose.

She smiled at the boy. He must have been six and ten at the most, impeccably dressed, and tailored into a jacket that was highly ornamented with symbols of stature. "You are messenger to the seneschal of Inara?"

He straightened. "Indeed, miss." He held the letter out in a gloved hand and, evidently realizing he'd stopped several paces short, sort of hopped forward to reach her.

Nim pressed her lips together and adamantly refused to let her gaze slip toward Allister, who watched from near the doorway. She cleared her throat. "My, that is quite a station for one so young. Tell me, does the seneschal employ many personal messengers?"

The boy's brows drew together. "He said you'd try to wiggle information out of me."

"Wiggle?"

"Aye," the boy said. "'A woman like her will be wilier than you give her credit for.'"

Nim crossed her hands in her lap. "I wonder that he should give me any credit at all with that sort of talk. 'A woman like me?'"

The boy winced.

"I suppose he expected you not to repeat that bit." At his silence, she shifted forward in her chair and gave him a conspiratorial smile. "No bother. We'll keep that just between us."

His cheeks flushed but only for a moment before his eyes narrowed. By all appearances, he was not fooled by her attempts at charm.

Nim held a hand forward. "Will you be my messenger each time?"

He nodded. "I'm the only one for the seneschal's personal correspondence." Then his gaze shifted, as if realizing he'd given her the answer to her previous question quite by mistake.

"Good," she said. "I like you. Now, give me your name and let Allister show you to some tea while I decide if a reply is necessary."

"Wesley," the boy said. "And I'm to wait here, as there will most certainly be a response."

Nim's brow rose, and she finally fell to the temptation of glancing at Allister. She wished she hadn't. "Tea," she managed.

"Of course, my lady."

Allister bowed grandly before escorting the boy from the room, leaving Nim alone with her thoughts and a letter from a man who was second to only the king. "For all that is sacred," she muttered. She might have laughed had the letter not been so heavy in her hand. She glanced at it, pale against the folds of her dark skirt.

The seneschal's elegant hand was slanted across what might have been the finest parchment Nim had ever held. *The notable Lady Weston, Hearst Manor.* She blinked. *Notable.* She supposed it wasn't an insult, though it was probably best not to think on the word for long.

She ran a finger over the letter's seal, a dagger and an annulet on a shield beneath a phoenix, pressed into dark-red wax. It cracked loose, and she examined the ribbon beneath it more closely, half certain it had been made from the same material as her missing cloak.

Nim unfolded the parchment, dreading what awaited her inside.

My Lady,

Please do not abuse poor Wesley. I have grown quite fond of him and would prefer to keep him on. By now, you've had time to consider our agreement and have settled with the idea as best you can. As such, the days spend quickly toward the turn of the moon. Submit to me a full report of your last encounter with your keeper, as well as any tokens that have been passed to you by the society.

With Regard,
—W

NIM STARED AT THE WRITING, dumbfounded. She remembered the boy's words about there *most certainly* being a response and frowned. She stood, her previous notes and trappings fluttering to the ground, forgotten, and crossed to the small writing desk near the window. Taking pen and ink to hand, she scratched out a loose note.

My esteemed lord W, held in highest of regard, ~~even by himself,~~

Thank you for your favor. I'm referring, of course, to the letter and the use of your darling boy. I am quite overwhelmed by your generosity in allowing me a full morning to recover, as well as your concern for my health. One can only hope that your fears will be eased by the assurance that I'm not fool enough to relay information of this private—dare I say intimate—a matter in such a common manner that might put my own health and the health of our beloved Wesley at risk.

With Discretion,
Your reluctant agent

NIM FOLDED her message and gathered the most important of her papers and books to carry to her own desk, where she sealed the letter with wax quite hastily before returning to find Allister and the boy. Young Wesley was half full of cakes, his gloves in a pile on the floor.

"Miss—my lady," he said around a mouthful of delicate pastries.

She waved off his attempt at a bow. "I've managed a response." When she held the letter forward, he reached for it, and she caught sight of his mangled hand. Her intake of breath was sharp, and he flinched away, but Nim only stepped closer. "What happened to your hand?"

"It's nothing miss. I—"

"Does he punish you? Does that bullheaded—"

The startled noise that came from the boy drew her up short. "That's treason, miss." His words were a whisper. Nim crossed her arms, and he added, "It's not what you think. It's not him at all. Lord Warrick has never raised a hand to me. He's treated me nothing but well."

Nim's narrowed gaze trailed the lines that ran into his sleeve. "I'm no fool about wounds, Wesley. I can see that this damage was not the fault of a single accident. These scars are none the same age." He'd been tortured, repeatedly, and it appeared that the jagged, hot red scars had been left by someone with magic—someone like an agent of the Trust—who'd stolen as a sacrifice payment for its cost. "I know who the seneschal is, and I know how this type of wound is made."

The boy's eyes went round. "You know Warrick? Truly? He said you'd only just met." He looked a little crestfallen. "He said he wouldn't lie to me."

Guilt pinched Nim's heart. She uncrossed her arms. "He hasn't lied. We did just meet. I only mean I know the type of man he is." The associations he kept, at least. What he looked like in a thin linen shirt. She cleared her throat before attempting a softer tone. "He didn't do this to you?"

"No, my lady. I swear. It was like this... from before." He glanced at Allister. "I'm not supposed to talk about it."

She stepped forward and patted his shoulder. "Of course, you're in the right. It was exceptionally rude of me to ask. I was only worried for you." She understood his tone. The Trust had hurt him. The marks that remained would hurt him still—it was what the sacrifice was. Permanent. Painful. A trade for what the magic had wrought. The boy was not to speak of it. It would cost him more than his position as messenger. It would cost his life. She set the letter on the table beside him. "Have Allister pack up some cakes for you, hmm?"

A sheepish grin changed the boy's face. "I'm very loyal to Lord Warrick, and he does treat me quite well..."

Nim smiled. "But he doesn't give you cakes." At the boy's nod, Nim looked to Allister. "Alice-sized rations for this one, my good man."

CHAPTER 10

The second letter came while Nim was still in bed.

"My lady," Allister said in a tone that suggested it was not the first time, "you have an urgent message."

Nim grumbled and pushed to sitting, the light between the curtains indicating it was the small hours before dawn. "All things sacred. What sort of pompous clod—" She narrowed her eyes. Allister narrowed his own right back. "Is Wesley in the room with us?" Nim whispered.

"Absolutely not," Allister assured her. "Propriety would never allow such a slight."

There was a long silence before Nim said, "He's just outside, isn't he?"

"Attached to the door, it would seem."

Nim groaned and fell back onto the bed.

"Shall I fetch your robes, my lady?"

"No bother." She sighed. "I might as well dress for the day. After all... what day is it, Allister?"

"A day past yesterday, my lady. We'll be waiting in the corridor."

After drawing the curtains to let in the faintest glow of light, Nim picked up the candle he'd left as she scuffled toward the wardrobe. Lack of sleep complicated the process of dealing with buttons considerably, but she managed to dress before dawn broke through the windows. With a yawn, she pinned her dark hair back and made her way to the door.

Wesley was regaling Allister with tales of his employer. Nim set the candle by the door and leaned forward to listen through the thick slab of wood.

"...never seen him so ruffled. Thought he might call on her myself, I did. Don't think I'll leave here without a well-warranted response this time. No, sir."

Wesley straightened when Nim opened the door. Wearing a solemn expression, he made a grand bow. "A message for her ladyship, by order of the venerable seneschal of Inara, Lord Warrick Spenser, faithful to his duty, honorable beyond question, and... not terrible to look at."

Allister's face remained impossibly serene. Nim pressed her lips together. "Does he make you say all of that to all of his intended recipients?"

"Oh no, my lady. I'm only to sound official. I get to make the last bit up at will." He pulled a face. "It's a mite tricky past the first parts."

Nim grinned. "I would imagine, though I'm certain he would be mightily impressed by the job you've done."

Wesley seemed to shake himself, thrusting a folded parchment toward her. "The message."

"Thank you, Wesley. Please, let Allister provide you some tea and cakes while you wait."

His eyes lit up, and though otherwise composed, Nim thought she might be able to win him over. Not from the seneschal, maybe, but at least so that he might ease into conversations that would help her case. She gripped the thick parchment in her hand and made her way to the sitting room, where the first light of dawn cut across the city beyond and into the gentleman Hearst's plush rooms.

The ink on the letter was hastily done, and the address... *Her ladyship, the remarkable Nimona Weston.*

"Remarkable," Nimona murmured. It somehow seemed not an improvement. She ran a finger over the black ribbon, cracked the seal, and unfolded the parchment. A familiar woody scent rose to her, reminiscent of myrrh and balsam. He must have written it just before calling for Wesley, must have held it in his hands no more than an hour before. Nim realized she had raised it to her face to better detect the scent. She jerked it away, horrified at herself, before glancing over her shoulder.

The room was empty, so she leaned against the windowsill with a shake of her head then held the message toward the light.

My lady,

Be assured that you misunderstand the agreement that binds you. As my agent, your actions are mine to call. These are not suggestions but orders. Further, your doubts regarding our correspondence are misplaced. Trust that a man of my station would know well enough whether young Wesley was safe transport of any intimate messages you wish to send. I will not repeat my request; you know what is required of you. I expect it before another day passes.

Regards,
—W

NIM STARED at the sharp lines of the W and the depth at which it was etched into the page. She'd gotten under his skin—that was clear. But he was a fool if he thought she would lay bare her secrets for all the world, set her neck on the block, and hand Calum an axe. Her finger tapped against the thick paper, then she found her feet moving quite without having decided how best to act.

"Wesley," she snapped as she entered the small nook near the kitchen. His head shot up, his cheeks packed with pastry. Allister stood watchfully, though she imagined he'd been perched on a stool in a friendly manner before he heard her footsteps. The muffled clatter and rustle of early-morning kitchen chores came from beyond a set of double doors. Nim bit the edge of her lip. "Is the seneschal not busy with kingdom duties all day? If I send a reply, will he be able to get away from those duties—should it be urgent, I mean?"

The boy swallowed a lump of food. "Yes, my lady. Lord Warrick, he's a very busy man. Though he could get away, I suppose, should the business at hand be more urgent than that of the king."

Nim held the letter to her chest. "Tell him I understand."

"My lady?"

"My response," Nim said. "Tell the seneschal my response is 'I understand.'" She wasn't convinced it would buy her the time she needed to think, but certainly, he could not simply walk from his post without alerting the king. He could, she specu-lated, simply tell the king's men she was a thief or that she was tied to the Trust. It would be very easy for a man of his station to do away with the lady Nimona Weston completely. But Warrick needed something from her. He must have. Otherwise, he would never have let her live at all.

Wesley's look was doubtful. "I beg your pardon, my lady, but I'm not certain that was the sort of reply the seneschal was looking forward to."

"Hmm." Nim tapped a finger to her lip. "You're likely right." She glanced up at Allister. "Do send some cakes along for the seneschal as well. I'd hate terribly to disappoint someone as respected as Lord Warrick."

Wesley's gaze slid from Nim to Allister then back. "My lady..."

Nim settled onto the stool across from him. "What is it, Wesley? Does the seneschal not like cake?" She frowned. "What would he have, then? Does he have a special interest? A hobby, perhaps? What is it that our Lord Warrick enjoys?"

A stillness came over Wesley, then he slid the cake plate forward, away from himself and Nim, evidently aware that he was being plied with baked goods and polite conversation. "He is very interested in whether his orders are properly carried out. He enjoys gentlemen and ladies who show a deference to duty." His hazel eyes were sharp. "He expects respect, my lady. Honorable intentions."

A coldness swam through Nim. She drew her fingers back from the table. "And what if I don't do as he expects, Wesley?" She glanced at his hands, the tip of his finger gone beneath a fine pair of gloves and who knew what else beneath his jacket and shirt. "Will I lose a part of myself? Will I be scorched by magic?"

The color drained from Wesley's face, but he did not look away. "I've told you before, that was not Lord Warrick."

"Even so. Why should I trust that he will not do such a thing to me?"

The boy did not flinch or answer that it was because Warrick *had* no magic, which meant he knew. Allister was as still as a wall beside him, but Wesley, apparently showing more trust to him than to Nim, did not even glance the man's way.

"My father did this." The boy's voice was suddenly younger but more certain than it had yet been. "He bargained, and he lost."

A sick feeling rose from Nim's belly, and she tasted something copper on her tongue. "It was wrong of me to press you, Wesley. I'm sorry. Truly." She'd brought it up again, knowing full well how it had affected him. The boy was not the first she'd seen scarred. Signs of the Trust were everywhere, the scars only a piece of the evidence, sacrifices required so that the Trust could draw on the energy, bend it to their will, and bestow it upon those who did not bear magic. They had to pay the toll.

It was only that she needed to know and be certain she was not risking the same—she couldn't allow herself to be punished by magic again.

Her gaze dropped, unable to look at Allister when she admitted to a stranger something she'd never discussed with someone she considered a true friend. It was a horrible, dark, and ugly thing, her secret. The best would have been to leave it buried, but buried things sometimes rose through the earth, bringing even darker trouble along with them when they came.

"My father has done the same." Beneath the table, her hands clenched into fists. "And I shall never forgive him."

The room was still and silent for several long moments before it was broken by Wesley's whisper, his answer to her fears. "My lady." When Nim looked up, he said, "It was the seneschal who saved me from them."

CHAPTER 11

Nim was convinced she was about to be hanged. Warrick had likely sent soldiers out for her hours before. She couldn't say she wasn't concerned, but she would rather be hanged—tortured, even—than surrender to the Trust.

She'd made up her mind: Warrick was the lesser risk. Warrick was the one person who might have information to help her find a way free. Decision in hand, she was marching straight to the doom of her choosing.

Wesley had said that Warrick had saved him but refused to reveal much else. It had been a tightly held secret with good reason. A contract with the Trust could not simply be bought with money or jewels. It took sacrifice—personal sacrifice, torn from its victim with great pain to feed the magic.

Nim hadn't seen anyone actually escape the Trust without great cost. And while she supposed there had been great cost paid by Wesley, given his wounds, he had still managed to secure a position in society, and near a king, no less. The boy seemed satisfied and well adjusted, as if he might someday be just Wesley and not the contract that had bound him.

Warrick had done that.

Nim was no fool. She knew there would be risk. Calum had

assigned the seneschal, a man who had evidently beaten the Trust's game, as Nim's task. She could not know what her keeper had planned, but Warrick Spenser was second to the king and enemy to the Trust.

Nim was decided.

The shadows were black as pitch against a sky that showed no hint of dusk or dawn. It was late enough that should she be caught, she would not be able to talk her way out of it, but Warrick had at least given her a path concealed from the guards inside the castle. Once she made it into the hidden passageway, she would be safe—safe as she might have any chance to be. Wesley had said that when the seneschal was angry, he'd nearly called on Nim himself. She could not let such a thing happen. There would be no way to hide a visit to Hearst Manor from Calum and the Trust.

So she had come to Warrick instead.

He'd set a deadline in his message, *before another day has passed*, but Nim would give him what he'd asked for by the end of the night. She held the lantern high, letting the warm glow of its magic illuminate her path down the hidden corridor. Nim prayed no one else used the passage but was fairly certain the seneschal would not be fool enough to allow anyone to find a corridor secreted by magical means, let alone with access to his rooms. A man of his station would have had a price on his head—a price, it seemed, that would happily be paid by the Trust.

The panel came open into the very room she'd left the night he'd caught her, when he'd trapped her between himself and the desk, but this time, no moonlight came through the massive row of windows. Her heart picked up, her nerves suddenly on edge at the rash actions that had driven her through the city once she had made her decision. She had not been invited. She'd stolen into his private rooms again. She was wrong about not being a fool. Worse, it seemed she was a fool with a death wish.

Nim settled the lantern in its alcove then carefully entered the room. The warm glow of candlelight flickered from beneath the opposite doorway, and she had a moment of panic that he might be hosting guests. She backed up a pace, but she'd come so far already. There was no reason not to listen at the doorway, to quietly cross the room and, should he be entertaining, quietly leave again—no reason aside from that it was eavesdropping.

"Curse it," she whispered, striding into the darkness with a purpose, despite all natural sense and wit.

She was nearly halfway across the room when a third door opened. Nim staggered to a stop, gaping at the hulking figure in the doorway. He crossed his arms over an entirely shirtless chest and stared back at her with a dark look.

"I—" Nim held up a finger as if it was somehow going to lead her way out of the mess. It did not.

The seneschal stepped closer. "Lady Weston." His tone was strangely flat and unsurprised, given the situation.

"Wesley said—I, well, I've brought you information." She glanced nervously at the door behind him. "You're not... entertaining guests, are you?"

Warrick closed the door solidly, giving Nim only a glance of unidentifiable shapes in the darkness. The action forced him to uncross his arms, but his posture remained... *irritated?* She couldn't be certain.

She should apologize, surely, but she'd gone so far past any sort of decorum that she might as well have doused the actual king in pitch. She turned to face her observer. "My lord, while your assurances were adamant, I wish to report on the matter we discussed in person."

"The intimate matter?" His tone held something Nim could not identify. She might have thought he was toying with her had his posture not been so rigid.

"Yes. Regarding the information you requested and any tokens I'd been given."

"Well?"

She pursed her lips. "It will take more than a moment, I'm sure." His stare, shadowed as it was, seemed to imply that it would certainly take more than a moment, should she not just get on with it. His intimations were excruciatingly clear when he wanted them to be. "What I mean to say, my lord, is that you've time to... put on a shirt."

His chest flexed in a movement, catching a spare bit of light, and Nim's gaze strayed toward his form.

He stepped closer. "Miss Weston, you steal into my private rooms in the small hours of the night, question whether I'm entertaining guests, and expect me to be dressed for your company."

"I didn't—you misunderstand. I only mean to make you more comfortable."

"By invading my private quarters."

Nim huffed. "Well, I certainly cannot call on you in any way that is proper, now can I?"

His silence seemed to say, *and whose fault is that?*

She crossed her own arms, stung by his assessment. "Have you something against light in this room?"

The clouds took it upon themselves in that moment to part, letting half a dozen shafts of moonlight spear through the window and, to her horror, over the lines of his chest. Heat rose in Nim's cheeks, and she had to resist the urge to back away from him. Not because she wanted to but because she very much didn't. She wanted to look at him, which would have been incredibly foolish.

He was the seneschal of Inara, second to the king and the man responsible for hanging people like her.

Nim's hands curled into fists. She couldn't help it. She'd always been drawn to magic, pulled by a horrible desire to reach for it. To brush against it—*him*, in this case.

Her eyes managed to stay on his for a moment, but when he drew a breath, her gaze betrayed her, falling over the curve of his shoulder and onto the plane of his muscled chest. Near his shoulder was a jagged scar, like so many wounds she'd seen left by the Trust.

Her finger twitched with the irrational urge to touch it, even as something inside her warned her to step back. She could almost imagine the way the scar would feel beneath her finger-tip, still warm, still painful, holding some lingering sense of the magic that had marked it in the first place.

Her gaze shot to his, and an unspoken message told her not to ask. "You said you wouldn't lie to me," she said.

"That does not mean I have to answer your questions."

She wanted to tell him she knew about Wesley, that the boy had confessed. But it was not her secret to tell—it was between Wesley and Warrick. Then again, it was clear there was far more to Warrick and the Trust than her task. She would find out what it was and discover if it could in any way help her get free.

"My lady," he said, "while I cannot say I am not intrigued by your nighttime romps through my private rooms, they remain the only hours of the day where I am free to attend personal affairs."

"Oh," she said. "Of course." *Get on with it, Nim. Just tell him the whole sordid tale.* "Shall we sit down?"

A single brow raised at her continued delay.

She cleared her throat. "I paid my last tithe at the turn of the moon." It was not the bit of information she'd been afraid to convey in a hastily scrawled message, sent with a boy who'd been scarred by magic. What was more, it was information Warrick likely already knew.

In fact, he knew far more about her than she liked. Her gaze strayed over his hair, unmussed despite the hour. It was dark, a shorter style but not recently cut, though his square jaw appeared just shaven. Shadows cut his face into sharp angles, the line of his nose, the dip of his brow.

He was handsome, just as Margery had said. But something in his bearing made him more than simply pleasant to look at. She felt an unsettling urge to move closer.

"Miss Weston."

Nim snapped out of her perusal, and her cheeks flushed as

she forced her gaze to the floor. But though she could feel his intentions and sense the power within him, Warrick was not Calum. He wasn't like the others she'd been exposed to through the Trust. She let her eyes return to his. They did not capture her. They did not freeze her into place.

"Is it because it's so dark?" Her words slipped out unbidden.

Warrick's brows drew together.

"The reason you can't—" *Snare me like a rabbit.* She waved a hand. "Never mind. I reported to pay my tithes and was tasked with retrieving the watch from you." She did not remind him that she'd intended to drag the month out by extorting an agent of the king, though Warrick had certainly not forgotten. She stepped forward, reaching into the pocket at her waist to retrieve the only token she'd ever been gifted by an agent of the Trust. Warrick's gaze fell to her hand, then briefly lowered to her unfit-for-proper-society pants. She thrust her hand toward him. "This is it, all I have."

He reached to take the locket from her palm then turned it over. The silver flashed in the moonlight, strange etchings that resembled ivy and thorns and something of a snake carved over its surface. Something told her Warrick recognized the design. His voice was strange. "You don't wear it?"

"Stones, no."

He looked up at her.

"I keep it hidden beneath a pile of blocks outside the manor. You think I'd sleep with that thing around my neck?" Not when the Trust could choke her with it. Not when Calum's thoughts had strayed so near the feeling of a chain around her neck that she'd nearly been ill as she stood right in his chamber. A shiver ran over her. "I won't even bring it inside my rooms."

"Why bargain for this if you've such a distaste for it?"

He'd straightened to look at her, and when she flinched at his words, it seemed as if she might have been flinching away from him. Her indignance at his comment kept her from correcting that assumption. "I did not bargain for that thing." She shook her head. "I told you, I don't bargain."

His fingers tightened around the locket. "He gave this to you without a bargain."

"Yes. You said you wanted any tokens I'd received. This is it, only this."

A roiling sensation rose through Nim, followed by a strange sort of heat. She stared at Warrick. "What is it?" she asked.

The clouds closed, throwing his green eyes once more into shadow. His voice was ice in contrast to the strange heat that had Nim wanting to throw off her jacket. "The society doesn't give anything without a bargain. Nothing is without cost."

Her throat went dry. "I made no agreement. I bargained nothing. I didn't even want the fool thing."

The locket made a thin metallic crunch inside Warrick's closed fingers. He tossed it into the hearth, and a hot flash of magic lit the darkness, his power burning the locket to ash. "Nothing is without cost."

CHAPTER 12

Nim stared at the seneschal of Inara where he stood, shirtless and seething. The locket he'd just melted without as much as glancing inside had come from Calum. Her keeper had forced her to take it when she'd been snared by his gaze, long ago.

Something dark and terrifying snaked through her, and Nim did not think she could tell Warrick about the incident, even had she wanted to. She did not want to, though, because she could see the effect it had on him and could sense it rolling off of him.

The burst of power strong enough to liquefy metal had not quelled the magic inside him. He felt dangerous and deadly, but Nim did not fear those sensations. She could tell they were not meant for her. She may not have trusted Warrick, but it seemed she'd found an ally against the Trust, and she had no intention of wasting it.

"That's that, then." She wiped a palm over her thigh. "So, I take the drum watch and—"

He gave her a look that said not to test him.

Nim shrugged.

"Wesley," he snapped. The door to the sitting room swung

open, and Nim startled away from the light and the shirtless man beside her.

Wesley, fully dressed—she thanked the fates—stumbled bleary-eyed through the doorway to stand at attention. "Nim," the boy said cheerily when he became alert enough to take her in.

Warrick's gaze shot from Nimona to Wesley.

Wesley cleared his throat and managed a stately bow. "Your ladyship."

Nim bit her lip. "Wesley. Working day and night, I see."

His expression turned wary as he glanced at Warrick. "No, my lady. Or, I suppose, not usually."

Warrick abandoned his obvious scrutiny of the exchange between his assistant and his intruder. "His tasks have picked up considerably since you've come into the picture, Miss Weston." Wesley gave Nim a private smile, and Warrick added, "He doesn't seem to mind, given that you've kept him in supply of an obscene number of pastries and cakes."

Warrick drew a piece of parchment to the center of his desk and tapped the quill in ink. Nim and Wesley both stood silently, watching the steady curve of the quill, the smooth glide of Warrick's hand. A perverse part of Nim wanted to step closer, to watch the letters form despite the fact that he was writing corre-spondence she'd not been invited to view. She waited for the scratch and swoop that accompanied his W then shifted her gaze back to the boy.

Warrick stood, folding the paper as he crossed to Wesley, not bothering with wax. Wesley gave his employer a swift nod followed by a more polite one aimed at Nim. "Please tell Allister the answer is seven and ten."

"Certainly," Nim said.

There was a flash of candlelight as Wesley exited through the sitting room, and when the door closed behind him, Warrick crossed his arms.

"What?" she said. "I have no idea what is *seven and ten*. The two leave me entirely out of the conversation most times."

"You've known the boy for two days. Am I to believe your entire household has taken him to their bosom already?"

"Of course not." She waved an arm. "He's not even met young Alice yet."

Warrick's answering expression was flat. Nim didn't mind, because the dangerous edge was gone from his emotions, the swimming heat simmering well out of reach. He leaned against the desk with his long legs crossed and his wide, bare chest edged in shadow. She had the distinct impression that she'd quite accidentally become overly familiar with the venerable Lord Warrick as well.

"I should go," she said.

"Yes." He reached beside him on the desk and picked up a letter that had already been written. He gestured with the parchment. "Your instructions."

"My—" Nim stepped forward. He had told her plainly how it would be. His commands were just that. She would do as she was bid. She wet her lips then took the letter from his hand.

He did not move from his relaxed position, and she did not steal more than a glance at the correspondence scattered over his desk. The air between them was still, and yet the strange sensation that she could not quite decipher charged the space. She gave her hands a task, opening a missive that was surely meant for her to read once she was gone. It was short, like an order Calum might have given her, and before she even read it, she muttered, "I see the pleasantries have gone."

"And you were so good at them," Warrick murmured.

She gave him a look from beneath her lashes before she read the note.

Seventh corridor. Eighth door. First cabinet. Third drawer.

SHE STARED at him at eye level, since he was relaxed against the desk. He did not flinch. She dropped her hands, the letter brushing the thin mace strapped to her thigh. "No."

Warrick sighed deeply, readying himself, she supposed, for some unpleasant task. Possibly, it was to drag her to the king. Possibly, it was their continued conversation when they both should clearly have been in bed.

Their own beds, obviously.

"No," she said again. "I'll not do it. You don't understand. I hate it there. *Hate*. There's no reason that I should do this and no way you can make me and—"

"Nimona." His voice was low, held something of a purr, and somehow managed to be both weary and a threat. "You know very well what our bargain entails. You know there will be risk. You know that there is very good reason you should do this and that I unequivocally can make you." He leaned forward. "You are intimately aware of the alternative."

Nim swallowed. She was too much at ease in the man's presence. She kept forgetting he was not just the seneschal of Inara, not just a man from whom she'd attempted stealing and who was second to the king. Warrick was something else, as well, something far more dangerous. Warrick had magic. Warrick could make her.

"I won't like it," she whispered in a vaguely petulant hiss.

"I won't, either."

His words stunned her along with a sense that they were entirely true. And something else. Regret, maybe. Reluctance. Her own words slipped free without her intent, her fingers refolding the letter nervously. "Why can I feel so much from you? Why can I sense things here that I cannot at the Trust?" *Why am I not terrified?*

He pushed himself to standing, and they were suddenly very

near one another. The power in his presence was undeniable, and Nim had always found herself drawn to magic in the worst possible way—with a desire to touch it.

"I told you," he said, his tone once more a vow. "I'm bare to you."

CHAPTER 13

Nim made the hastiest of retreats, excusing herself from the seneschal's company to flee into the night like a raging coward. She was halfway through the kingdom before she realized he'd likely intentionally done it to scare her off. What exactly he'd done she wasn't certain, but Nim had distinctly felt something more than just his presence warm and close before her, half of it blatantly bare. She cursed, forcing herself not to dwell on that particular bit. She was a fool if she let herself be drawn to a man of his station. It could only end badly or worse.

She still could not wrap her mind around the fact that someone with access to magic was living above ground, outside the Trust, and as a citizen of Inara. Worse, right under the king's nose. Clearly, the seneschal was hiding his secret, but Nim didn't know exactly what it meant, only that she'd tangled herself more deeply in dangerous affairs in her attempt to break free.

The sun was still hidden well beneath an unseeable horizon when she neared the manor, and Nim kept on, determined to have her foul task done with before cowardice reared its head again. She never visited the undercity if she could help it, but it was doubtful that anyone would take undue notice of her wandering the catacombs at such a late hour. Nim was familiar with only a few of the regulars and kept her affairs as private as possible. Besides, the place would be teeming with revelers, bettors who traded for favors from the agents of the Trust. They would be mindless with temporary pleasures, intoxicated by the possibilities, and up to entirely no good throughout the network of chambers and corridors.

She would be in and out before the sun rose. She had to be.

Nim slipped on her gloves and drew her cloak tighter around her shoulders, the rising wind tugging her hair loose from its binding. The coming day would be dreary and rain soaked, but should fate allow it, she would be back in her bed by dawn.

The gates to the undercity were raised, but the archway was poorly lit. It was hard to say whether the dim torches were because of an unusual draw on the magic or if it was owing to the small hours and the fact that no one leaving the gates come morning would want to be seen.

The guards gave her only a passing glance, but her palm brushed the hilt of her dagger beneath her cloak anyway. Weapons were permitted within the city, aside from possessing one near someone of Calum's station, and fights broke out frequently enough. But to take a life owned by the Trust meant to take on their contract, and Nim had no lives to spare. If worse came to worst, she would not be able to truly save herself. It was why she also carried a mace—to incapacitate without drawing much blood.

The entrance hall opened into a larger corridor, its stone walls rising high toward the arched supports beneath Inara. It was unsettling how quickly the corridors dived below the earth and how little aware one was of the incline until the sky had been replaced by dark stone. Metal cages hung overhead, chandeliers lit with magic, and the walls were bare of tapestry and art, making them even more imposing.

The undercity had been built with riches even if not a single coin had been spent. The best craftsmen, bound by the Trust and their magic, had toiled beneath the earth for lifetimes to escape the very contracts that had gained them their skill. The bettors never learned. The accounting never stopped.

Music, the sharp, crisp sound of a vielle, echoed from an adjoining chamber. The revelers, dressed in silks and fur, glimpsed through the open doorway, the air heady with a perfume of musk and spice. Nim held her breath until she was past it, aware from previous visits that she'd no interest in being recalled to the undercity every time she smelled the scents above ground. It was a perfectly excellent way to ruin a good meal. She hadn't eaten anything cooked with cloves for years. Not since her father.

Nim slammed the thought to the back of her mind, unwilling to call the memory forth with him locked below and the woman —who reigned as head of the Trust, whose magic was unfathomable in its strength—who'd done it so near.

Calum's mother would pass that power to him when he ascended to head of the Trust.

A lithe woman dressed in an Eastern style walked past Nim, her eyes clouded with blindness that did not seem to impede her progress in the least. Following her was a man in trim pants and a half mask, his shirt unlaced to the navel, his eyes glassy and his mouth twisted at the corner as if an especially charming thought had crossed his mind. Neither looked at Nim. No guards waited inside the undercity. No one paid her any mind.

Agents of the Trust could take care of themselves. The sentries present at the entrances of the tombs and Calum's chambers were only to remind those not under contract that the society was a business, that all was above board, and that those within the Trust were merely citizens of Inara.

None of it was true.

Calum and the others were nothing like honest or fair, and the penalty for even being below ground was as high as death. More than that, those of the Trust had a current of power running through them, energy that swelled from a source deep within the undercity, fed their magic, and made them capable of manipulating both physical matters and fates. They were not normal residents of the kingdom. A person was either born with magic or not. Citizens of Inara were not.

But the Trust had other varieties of manipulation, such as the ability to snare with just a look and the strange sensation that told Nim when she was in danger because of the ideas running through her keeper's head. She disliked that the most.

A jovial singsong echoed through the hall behind her, but Nim did not look back. Calling attention to oneself was a solidly bad choice in the undercity and singing aloud especially so. Besides, she was counting the corridors and had finally made her way to seven. She drew a needed breath as she turned to enter a narrower and more dimly lit passage. The first door was carved with symbols, the second and third ornate with trim. There was nothing particular that stood out about the eighth.

As she glanced over her shoulder to be certain she was alone, she prayed that the room on the other side was not filled with revelers of any sort. Brushing away the reminder that Warrick had taken her key and with the knowledge that nothing in the undercity seemed to be locked—no one was fool enough to steal from the Trust—she reached out. Her gloved hand was on the dark lever before she realized it was not metal but bone.

She barely held in a noise of revulsion, her body shuddering in a single involuntary spasm. The door came open to a dark room, stale with still air and apparent disuse. Nim went back into the corridor to fetch a light then carefully closed the door behind her.

In the flicker of the torch, she saw that not only the lever was bone. The frame was trimmed in a tilework of shards, each chipped and worn or nicked from teeth. She backed away from the entrance, turning slowly to take in the room. It was filled with rows of cabinets and seemed to be nothing more than storage, which eased her concern that she might happen upon revelers but raised her hackles. Should she be caught, she would have no good excuse.

A dozen cabinets stretched along the near wall, their row disappearing into the shadows, with another row against the opposite wall and several centering the room. "What the deuce is the first cabinet?" she muttered, edging forward to check if they were somehow numbered. They were not. She silently cursed Warrick and turned a slow circle to take in more of the room. The torchlight caught on the bone framing the door, and beside it, a small cupboard with half a dozen drawers. Nim moved closer, uneasy at the import the cupboard seemed to carry. She glanced over her shoulder again at the rows of furniture, none of which seemed separated by style or size. It had to be the strangely carved cabinet made out of what she hoped was only animal bone.

She grimaced, reaching for the thing with an unsettling urge to squint to protect her eyes. The carved door opened to reveal more drawers. She counted to the third and was not surprised the pull was made of an animal tooth. The drawer slid open, its interior lined with velvet the color of ripe plums and a small gold coin lying at its center.

"A coin." Nim spoke as if her incredulous tone could reach the seneschal. But she was alone in the room. Even so, she could not quite make herself reach into the drawer to steal from the Trust.

She was trapped. There was nothing to do about that. Warrick had only come into her life days before, and yet anything he might do to her was categorically more preferable to what could come from the Trust. But he was asking her to commit a crime against them, inside their own home. *He found a way to free Wesley*, she reminded herself. Chest tight, Nim slipped her gloved fingers into the drawer, drawing out the coin while touching as little of the velvet as possible. She closed the cabinet and tucked the coin into the pocket that lined her boot shaft. She did not like something belonging to the Trust touching her, did not like being underground, and did not like breathing their air. Nim was ready to get out. She glanced around the room to be certain everything was intact.

Laughter rang through the hallway outside, and Nim froze. Muffled voices drew closer, raising the fine hairs at the base of her neck. The voices did not stop—they were, in fact, drawing still nearer. In a panic, Nim closed a gloved hand over the torch then hissed in pain when the magic-bought flame didn't extinguish.

Footsteps sounded outside the door. There was muted shuffling and conversation. Someone was about to come through.

She pressed the torch onto the stone floor, but it would not go out. She left it there and slowly crept backward, turning to run the moment the door started to shift.

She was in the darkness near the back of the room in a heartbeat, unable to see anything before her and unable to bear looking back. Her feet slowed as she ran her hands over the faces of the cabinets to find her way. She prayed her gloved palms would not touch something soft, something human, or anything at all that was not cabinet or wall. The voices at the front of the room had gone terribly silent, and she was certain they were aware of an intruder, given the lit torch on the floor. It was not the most preferable way to go, being caught in a storeroom and stealing a trinket she did not even want, but when whoever was in the front of the room picked up the torch and spread that light toward her, she was done for—seen and caught.

Her fingers slid from cabinet to air, and she moved sideways, finding the wall behind it. The stones led her farther into the darkness, and she exhaled a grateful breath when her palm slid over a door. She located the lever and pushed, running full speed through the corridor when she realized it was lit and would likely alert whoever had been in the dark storage room that she'd left. She had no idea where she was. She only ran, imploring fate at each turn that she would head the right direction.

More voices echoed from the end of the passage, and Nim spun to enter another closed door. Three people in the room glanced up, but she supposed a panting, frantic woman running through the halls was nothing particularly out of the ordinary there. She straightened, shrugging her cloak into order, and crossed the room to the opposite door. There, she found another passage, somehow grander and more intimate at once. Nim glanced in each direction then chose the more brightly lit one. She needed to find the main hall. She needed out. Above ground. *Home*.

She wasn't near the main hall and could tell as soon as she saw the first door. The wood had been etched with great symbols carved into relief of writhing animal forms. Her heart picked up speed in her chest as some sick part of her wanted to reach out, run her fingers over the wood, and brush against the magic. The stone beneath her feet was polished, each tile massive and twisted. The shapes, she realized, were not animals at all. They were more human.

Her feet paused over the stone before stepping sideways, nearer the wall. The hallway seemed alive. She must have been closer to the depths of the undercity, to the queen and her lair. Nim had made a terrible decision, over all, and she was not quite certain how exactly she might get out of it. She felt the coin within her boot, the fool thing seeming to burn her flesh though it was not hot at all. It was only her imagination, but her guilt and the evidence could do her in. She should toss it into a pit. She would as soon as she found one.

Nim paused before another doorway, the form etched into it giving the impression it was moving, beckoning her in. An eerie sound echoed through the corridor behind her, and though good sense was urging her to walk away, Nim's feet shifted toward the door, easing her forward with the stealth of a cat on the hunt. She lay a gloved palm on the wood. The door crept open a fraction, a slit of glowing amber light begging her to look. She shouldn't. She knew she shouldn't.

Reason didn't stop her. The magic was too strong. Nim's head angled to peer through the slender crack at the masked figures inside. Men and women, their sinuous forms in liquid silk, lay draped over stone sculptures situated around some sort of spring. Steam rose from the darkness of the spring, its surface like water in the black of night. Candles burned in clusters, not by magic, but dripping with foul tallow. Heat came through the doorway, and that woody, spicy scent of cloves returned. Nim's stomach swam, and she moved to back away. But one of the figures turned, his dark eyes finding hers through the door and sparking with recognition.

Nim's breath fell out of her in a curse. And then she ran.

CHAPTER 14

Nim's feet were not fast enough. They could not be. No matter if she made it out of the Trust, Calum had seen her.

It did not stop her from running. She sprinted through the corridors, taking endless turns that all seemed wrong, and then finally—*finally*—came into the main hallway that led to the gate. She did not stop running until she neared the entrance and its guards. They might already have known. They might have been waiting for her.

Her hand found the dagger beneath her cloak. There was only one way out. Nim held her head high, refusing to look back to see whether Calum was coming for her. She strode through the archway, the guards turning to glance at her but not stopping her. She did not know if they intended to give chase. The Trust liked to hunt their prey, to give them a bit of string so they might think they were getting away. The wind grabbed at Nim's hair as her pulse hammered through her. She resisted, at least until she reached the first alleyway toward the city, the urge to run and entice them.

Nim's boots paced faster than they'd ever gone the moment she cleared the guards' view. She might have thrown that cursed coin away had it not required her to stop, because there was no way she was brave enough—foolish enough—for that. She kept on the entire way back to Hearst Manor. Had she some safer place to go, she would have gone there. But she didn't. Hearst was it. No place was safe from the Trust. She could never truly hide.

She slammed through the door to the hidden passage, heaving air in and out and staggering on weakened legs. Still, Nim did not stop until she was inside her room with the door secured behind her. Nearly collapsing on the floor, she stared at the entrance with her hands braced on her knees, knowing full well she did not have her key. She could not truly be safe there. Warrick had taken that.

Cursing the man, she used the last bit of strength in her trembling arms to shove the wardrobe in front of the door—not because it could keep out the Trust but because she'd nothing else she could do. The room was dark, but Nim found the basin then tore off her gloves to wash her hands and splash her face. She tossed her cloak onto the floor then crossed to the bed, afraid to remove her boots, afraid to take her eyes off the door.

Nim leaned against the wall in the corner, sliding down to sit on the floor as the wind picked up outside, battering against her windows in time with her heart. She watched the passage, waiting for whatever might come. Warrick had her key, the one bound with magic. There was no way to lock Calum out.

He would know she'd been in the storage room. Calum was no fool and would figure it out. What he would do about it Nim couldn't guess.

The coin was hot inside her boot. She did not touch it. She only sat, staring at the door.

The rain held, and the redness of dawn crawled across the floor of Nim's room, slowly catching her bed afire then brightening to orange, lighting her chaise and the table before it. As it lightened again, going a yellow-white that burned Nim's bleary eyes, the door to her room opened.

Allister came in quietly, his gaze brushing past the untouched bedclothes to land on Nim in the corner. "My lady." His voice was careful, as were his steps, but he moved toward her anyway. Crouching in front of her drawn-up knees, he reached for Nim's hand. "Come out to the study."

She rose to follow him, and they stood side by side, Allister steadying her with an arm beneath her elbow. Alice met them in the corridor, tea tray in hand, her eyes darting between the lady Weston and the Hearst valet. She dipped a quick curtsy.

"To the study," Allister told the girl. "Best bring breakfast as well."

Alice nodded as she hurried to do as she'd been asked, and Nim shortly found herself settled in a bright corner of the reading room, surrounded by books that had no business being near her trembling hands with tea and food. She didn't bother with protest but only took what she'd been offered and tried to sort through the numbness that had settled through her bones.

"You've a guest," Allister told her. Her gaze rose to his. "Young Wesley," he explained.

Nim nodded. She was well enough for that, she supposed. If nothing else, it would get the fool coin from within her boot far away.

But as the warmth unfurled inside her from Allister's support, hot tea, and fresh biscuits, Nim's thoughts took on a less agreeable tone.

"Lady Weston." Wesley bowed deeply, his uniform in appropriate order and his mood seemingly at ease. His hazel eyes rose to hers. "I'm told you have something for Lord Warrick."

"No." The strength of her voice surprised even Nim. She was done playing the fool for men of power. Nim was not giving the coin up without a fight. Warrick would return her key, or she would toss his prize off the river bridge. "I've quite decided to deliver it myself."

Wesley flicked a glance to Allister, back to Nim. "My lady, Lord Warrick will be taken with seneschal business all day—"

"I won't bother him." She flicked a wrist as if swatting the idea away like a pestering gnat. "Sit, Wes. Have some breakfast."

"I thank you, my lady, but... well, you know he won't like this."

Nim curled her booted feet under her legs, still dressed in a wardrobe that would have given the head of the household an apoplexy. It didn't seem to bother Wesley. "I know you've been sent here to retrieve a package from me, but I take full responsibility. I will deliver it to him myself once I've had a chance to rest. Please tell him my message is that I'd like to inquire whether he might have time to see me tomorrow afternoon." A request for an official appointment would distract him, she hoped.

"Sit," Nim said again.

Wesley crumpled into the chair across from her.

Nim glanced at Allister, but he was already settling a plate beside their guest. "Wes, tell me about this purse provided by Lord Warrick."

He straightened. "Do you need supplies, my lady? I can—"

She shook her head. "Stay. I only want polite conversation. Just muse with me, won't you? What sort of fun things could we buy with such a purse?"

He gave her a wary look. "I've orders to provide whatever you ask for."

"Truly?" Nim could not help the smile that crossed her lips. "He warned you not to trust my words but gave you free rein to open the coffers?"

Wesley's concern was evident. "He did not expressly exclude any expenses..." He shook his head. "My lady, I'm certain..."

Nim chuckled. "Don't fret, Wesley. I'll not put you at risk. I'm only satisfying an indecent curiosity." It seemed an unreasonable leash. She had been caught in his rooms in the act of thievery, after all.

Wesley appeared to relax.

"Have you another appointment this morning?" Nim asked.

"No, my lady. Lord Warrick says I'm to be at your beck and call, that any fool can deliver his letters of state."

"Indeed." Nim grinned up at Allister. "Would you like to join us in a game of cards?"

CHAPTER 15

Nim spent the morning determinedly avoiding thoughts of what might come by playing cards with Wesley and Allister, picking at a late lunch while a storm raged outside, then sleeping fitfully the entire afternoon to the rumble of thunder and heavy wind. When she finally woke, her cheek plastered to the cushion of a sitting room chaise, she took a bath and avoided her rooms. But Elena was on the prowl, and Alice popped in to warn Nim of a formal dinner. She thanked the girl and made her way to her suite, hating that she'd nowhere to hide.

Nowhere to lock herself away.

She was trapped.

She didn't know if she had the patience to wait for a reply from Warrick, and, should she even receive it, what she might do with herself until the following afternoon. She paced her suite, miserable at the knowledge of a coming night, and finally, there was a knock on her door. Impatient, Nim crossed the room to jerk the door open, ready to tug a poor, drenched Wesley inside.

She lurched to a stop when she found Elena instead. Nim glanced nervously down the corridor, but the woman was alone. Maybe she'd caught Wesley at the entrance and sent him to the sitting room.

"Miss Weston." Elena's tone was strange, a shade off in what sounded as if it could be excitement, were that not entirely foreign to the woman's personality. She stared hard, forcing Nim to focus on her fine-featured face. "I've come to fetch you for dinner, your ladyship."

"Yourself?" Nim was too distracted for manners but tried to pull herself together. "I thank you, truly, but I'm not feeling well." She looked the part, in any case.

Before Nim was able to shut the door, Elena moved forward. "Miss Weston, you misunderstand. Your presence has been requested for dinner by from what I gather is an esteemed guest. He vows that he would value your presence, and I, as head of the household for Hearst Manor, must insist that you come."

Unease slithered through Nim's belly. But Wesley's words returned, how Warrick had threatened to come to the manor himself the last time she'd refused to do as he'd asked. It was him, surely, the seneschal of Inara. He had been so angry, Wes had said before. And now she had his coin. Nim swallowed her second refusal to go down for dinner, not wanting him to find his way to her room. "Thank you, Elena. I'll come just as soon as I'm dressed."

Elena's tone was level. "I'll wait."

Nim stared at her for a moment then gently closed the door. She shook herself and dipped her hands in the basin before splashing her face. After patting it dry, she sorted her hair into an acceptable knot and straightened the gown she'd put on earlier in the evening. It was not fit for a formal dinner with a guest who was second to the king, but Warrick had seen her in worse. She did not feel the need to impress him with jewels and brocade.

She opened the door to find Elena waiting as promised, and before the woman could give her wardrobe an appraising look, Nim said, "You'll have to choose between fancy dress or a delayed arrival."

Elena's eyes tightened just the slightest bit before she gave a sharp nod. The two paced silently through the corridor, the echo of Elena's shoes the only sound. The storm had quieted to a steady rain, and the halls were lit with ample tapers in honor of the formal dinner. Elena's shoulders were straight and stiff, and as she and Nim approached the door to the dining hall, Elena gave a small tug to the hem of her bodice, took a breath, then inclined her head to the men at the door.

Nim glanced over her shoulder, searching for Allister, but the doors to the dining hall opened, and conversation floated out to her. A strange coldness slid over her skin, snapping Nim's attention to the room and its voices as her feet, of their own accord, kept momentum through the doorway.

Three steps into the room, and the fool things abandoned her, rooting to the floor as all of the dinner guests turned in their seats toward the sound of distress that had crawled from her throat. All except for one, the man at the head of the table whose chair—whose eyes—were already turned in her direction, waiting.

Nim swayed, teetering between falling down and being sick. At the head of the gentleman Hearst's table, Calum smiled.

The chair beside him was being pulled out, the gesture clearly meant for Nim. They wanted her to take a seat beside Calum.

Across the table stood a small girl, her hair in perfect braids, her green eyes shaped into an emotion Nim could not pin down. *Alice.*

Calum was in her home, the place where Nim kept secrets and where she felt safest.

Allister. Her rooms. The hidden corridor. Nothing was safe from Calum.

"My lady." The gentle voice at her ear startled Nim, but it was only one of the staff trying to help her to her seat, because she was frozen in the middle of the room, making a scene of herself. He touched her elbow, and Nim jerked away, but she could not run. She could not leave Calum there, where he might hurt anyone. *Everyone*.

She forced her feet to move, to take her toward the head of the table and that proffered chair. Familiar voices picked up murmuring conversations, likely ladies and gentlemen concerned with the lady Weston's apparent attack of peculiarity, but she did not listen. She could not manage even the pretense of proper conduct as she perched on the edge of the chair beside her keeper.

Calum's eyes had never left hers, and the incongruity of seeing him in her home made the lines of his face seem somehow sharper, almost raptorial. "Lady Weston." His voice was a purr, evidence of his pleasure. Her reaction was everything he wanted—fear, obedience, the absence of composure. He wanted her to fall to the floor so that he might stand over her, press his cane to her sternum and—

Nim jerked free of the intimations coming from him with a shudder. She hissed, "What are you doing here?"

Calum's grin widened, his teeth on full display. It hurt to look at him. Because his look promised pain. "What am *I* doing here?" He laughed. "Nimona, you wound me."

His tone said something else entirely. It said, *I saw you*. It said she'd been caught inside his home. He wanted to know why. He wanted to play with her, to tease out the answer. Calum wanted to tell her what he would do once his cane was pressed to her chest.

Nim wanted nothing of the sort. She bit back her first two excuses. Calum was no fool. He would not be easily swayed. Whatever she told him had to be more than believable—he would be able to see agitation on her face. He had seen her run. She had to give him something he wanted. Too much time had passed when she finally answered. "I was curious," she said, "but I changed my mind."

Calum stared at her, and Nim let him have her gaze. She hoped it was a show of faith, that he would see it as her desire to share the truth or a sacrifice to save the people in the room. Nim wasn't certain it would work. She had no idea whose lives she risked. She dared not look away. Whoever sat at the Hearst table had put their safety in peril by coming. She could only pray that fate would see them through.

"You were curious," he repeated. His eyes narrowed on her, his tongue slipping over one side of his bottom lip. Nim shallowed her breathing and swallowed but left her gaze tangled with his. Nothing had ever felt so wrong. "Curious about our diversions." He steepled his fingers and dipped his chin near them to stare at her harder. "How very unexpected, Lady Weston."

Bile rose in her throat, and her palms broke with sweat. She was a fool with a wish worse than death. She was begging for torture from a man who knew it best, and for nothing. He owned her. There was no single way to be free.

He was in her home.

Nim forced her gaze not to flick away to find Allister, Alice, or any other face which might be in the room. It was all she could do for them: sacrifice herself.

"Yes." Calum's soft laugh echoed through the room, drowning out background conversation and bringing her focus solely to the sound. Calum laughing was never good, but suddenly, it felt like a knife to her heart. "So it will be," he said. "I will leave you to your fine dinner companions, Miss Weston, and you"—his dark eyes tightly drew the snare around her, constricting her breath and sending a fevered tremble through her limbs—"you will come to the undercity and experience our diversions for yourself." He smirked. "I'll send a messenger with the details."

NIM WAITED, trembling, in her room after Calum left. She was not certain what precisely she was waiting for until darkness fell and her feet were moving once more. She did not bother to change from the evening's gown, and her slippers became soaked within moments in the rain-drenched streets. It did not slow her but spurred her on. She was recklessly unafraid of who might witness what she meant to do. There were no secrets from Calum and the Trust. There was no place she might be safe. It was time to take it back.

She would win her freedom, even if she had to steal it.

She strode through the magic that concealed the secret entrance to the castle, disappearing into the darkness of the corridor. There was no way to know where the other corridors would take her should she turn from her course, but she needed not find out, because her feet remembered the way. The door at the end of the passage opened to Warrick's rooms, dark and empty with evening upon them but the depth of night still far away. The seneschal would be about the king's business, and Nim would have his suite to herself. She crept through the room, its windows inky with clouded sky.

Listening for movement, she let her eyes adjust to the darkness and searched out the narrow strips of space beneath the doors for any hint of light. There was none. Nim found a candle in the sitting room and lit it from the tinderbox. Her hands still shook, and though the downpour had stopped, she was damp through to the knees. The single flame provided enough light to find her way to the desk, but a thorough search revealed neither the key nor the drum watch. Nim straightened from her rummaging to stare at the room's only other door, where Warrick had come out shirtless the night before.

Crossing to it, she opened the door carefully then stepped into a room that felt strangely bare. Nim held the candle aloft to find a single small table, a chest of drawers, and a carved trunk at the foot of a low, wide bed. *Warrick's bedchamber.* A strange sensation rolled over her, and she drew her shoulders straight to shake it free. The room was bare of mirrors and art, of the bottles, brushes, and jars that scattered Nim's own room. She forgot for a moment that she was inside a castle and that every single item in his study and sitting room was elaborate, ornate, richly decorated.

His words came back to her. Those things were just for show, he'd said, gifts for a man who belonged to the king. Nim let her gaze trail slowly over the space before she returned to her task. She would find the watch. She would find her key. She would be done with the mess she was in before Calum saw her tortured and killed.

She placed the candle atop the chest of drawers then slid one open to search inside. No trinkets or keepsakes awaited her. The contents were utilitarian, trifles a man used in the course of cleaning and dressing for a position among court. She slid a second drawer open to find small clothes, thin linen, and stockings folded neatly in a row. Nim hesitated then opened the wide bottom drawer to see what waited there. Beneath a thin blanket was a longsword, its hilt carved and jeweled, its blade razor sharp. She ran a fingertip over the grip, wondering why she'd never seen Warrick with a sword on his hip. Surely, his station required it, and there in his barren rooms rested one of such high quality that it might have been a king's.

Nim shook herself, sliding the drawer closed once more. She had to have her key. It was the only way she could stay safe from Calum, even if it only provided enough respite to sleep.

She was elbow deep in the underthings of the venerable seneschal of Inara when she heard his voice.

"Miss Weston." The words were at once chiding and, Nim sensed, a bit staggered.

Had Nim been holding the candle, she might have very well burned down his room, but she only fumbled with soft linen she had no right to hold.

She spun to face him. "I need my key." The response came out before she'd had a moment to think. She was still shaken, angry, and feeling quite trapped. She was not repentant for being found in his personal... everything, but when she took him in, she was suddenly as awkward in his presence as she'd ever been.

Warrick was not shirtless but worse. He was wearing the long, dark robe, fine jacket, and tight, buttoned shirt of his post, seneschal of Inara, second to the king. His gaze raked over her, with her wild hair, bare arms, and trembling hands. And then lower, to where Nim's gown was soaked through the hem, dripping mud and street muck onto the seneschal's fine floor.

She felt chagrin, maybe, but still not sorry. She needed her key.

Warrick did not ask what had happened to her. A snap of magic knocked out the flame of her candle before he moved. When he reached for her, she was too stunned to back away, and she let him take her elbow to lead her out of his bedchamber. In the study, he placed her in front of a plush chair, glared her down to sitting, and removed his robe to lay it across her lap. The soft material smelled of him, that warm, woody scent, and still held the heat of his body.

Nim had not realized she was shivering with cold. Warrick crossed his arms and stared down at her, devastating in his uniform.

She pressed her lips together and swallowed hard. It wasn't as if she'd set out to be so entirely indecorous. She'd only... well, she'd had no other choice. "Calum," she told him. Her voice was raw and unsteady, her body trembling beneath the drape of Warrick's robe.

His gaze softened, and Warrick uncrossed his arms as he crouched before her.

"I need my key," she said. "It's the only"—a tremor racked her, breaking her declaration of its power—"way to keep him out."

A sensation passed from Warrick, but Nim could not decipher it since she'd become aware she was chilled to the core. Warrick sighed then reached beneath his cloak to slide Nim's drenched slippers free. He set them on the floor beside the chair, and Nim drew her bare feet beneath her inside the layers of her skirt.

Warrick stayed at the foot of the chair, his eyes an unsettling shade in the dim light. "The key can't help you."

Nim firmed her jaw. "You don't understand. It's not just a key. It's the only thing that can keep him out. If I'd had it tonight, he would never have come. He would have never been able to get inside to—"

A wave of nausea hit her as power swelled through the room so strong that she felt strange and dizzy and her ears begin to ring. She inched back from Warrick, into the thick arm of his sturdy chair.

"Calum came to you?" His voice was low and steady, but magic roiled inside him with an emotion Nim could not quite name.

"Yes," she said. "That's what I'm trying to tell you. You took my key, and now he can get in. I'm not *safe*."

Color rose above the buttoned neck of Warrick's collar, nearing his tight jaw. "You're wrong about the key."

Nim felt her own cheeks flush. "Then give it back. It's nothing to you."

Warrick's eyes narrowed on her. "But it is to you." He let his words simmer, keeping his gaze on her while she tried to work out what he meant. Evidently, he decided she wasn't clever enough for it, because he shook his head and stood. He turned, paced toward his desk, then faced her again. "It has kept him from you, but not in the way you think. The key you were promised and whatever they told you it would do... it never would have worked at all."

Nim felt her mouth go slack but could form no response, not when those promises had been so dear.

"He let you have the key because he knew you would grow attached to it. He knows what you prize and that allowing you to believe it was within reach would only make the key more precious to you." Warrick seemed to draw a steadying breath, and the magic in the room ebbed. "If you had faith that it afforded safety, the one thing he will never allow you, it would become strong enough to draw you to him and tie you tighter in those bonds."

Nim felt sick but not from the magic. It was the truth again, the conviction in Warrick's words. Her gaze took in his room, the trinkets he'd vowed meant nothing to him. She considered the warning that Calum believed he could find something to draw Warrick to the Trust. Warrick, with a bedroom that was bare, with nothing he valued enough to keep it safe.

The one thing she would never have, he'd said.

Freedom, Nim thought, was the thing she would never have. She would never be free.

"Why did you take it from me?" Her words were quiet in the stillness of the room, but Warrick did not answer. She knew the answer herself. He had taken it because it was true. Calum could have used it against her, and she'd had no idea.

Her mind returned to the locket that Warrick had burned in an empty hearth. Her key was probably destroyed, too, nothing more than ash.

Her gaze was somewhere distant, far removed from a dark room deep inside the castle that centered the kingdom of Inara. "You should have told me."

Another unidentifiable emotion swam over her from Warrick. His voice was calm, soft, but unapologetic. "I told you to bring me anything they gave you." He sighed. "It was my mistake to think it would have come directly from him."

Him. Calum. Warrick would not even speak the name. He knew their tricks far better than she. She was a fool, so far in over her head that she was already drowning. "Tell me what I can do."

"There's nothing you can do." Warrick turned from her to face the wide row of windows that centered the outer wall near the hidden corridor. Nim had never looked through the windows to anything but sky. She wondered what could be seen up close and what was below. She wondered how she'd gotten comfortable inside Inara Castle and so near a man of the king's, a man who could see her hanged. "I won't send you back there. I shouldn't have tried."

His tone seemed to imply that he shouldn't have thought she could do it, and even in her state of shambles, the sentiment stung. "It doesn't matter," she said. "I'm already going back." He turned to face her, and she muttered, "Against my will." Calum had caught her. The magic had drawn her despite her knowing better. Her shoulders slumped. "He saw me after I retrieved your coin."

Warrick stepped toward Nim, and she had the strangest sensation that he cared not at all about the coin. "Tell me what happened," he said. "All of it."

CHAPTER 16

Nim felt like the worst sort of fool. She'd thought the key was keeping her safe from Calum, even though she'd been using it when she'd been caught by someone else who held magic. She'd locked Warrick's door with it the first night she'd come there, but it had not kept him from her at all. It had been easy to believe that it hadn't protected her from him because she'd been inside his own rooms, because he'd come through the darkened corridor instead of the locked door, or because any other thing could be true, but she should have known. She should have suspected she would never be safe.

As she'd explained Calum's visit to Warrick, his magic had swelled through the room again. Something was wrong—something about Calum breaking rules, about things going too far—but Nim could only read what Warrick let slip past his defenses. He had vowed not to lie to her, but he'd been direct in stating that he had no responsibility to answer all of her questions.

It's over. I'm not safe, she'd planned to say. But Nim had never been safe at all. She'd only dug her hole deeper and, shovel in hand, had to return to Calum's lair.

"Is there no way I can protect myself?" Her words were no

more than a whisper, but she was strong again, any lingering coldness only in her heart.

Warrick had settled on the floor near the foot of her chair, one long leg drawn up with an arm draped over his knee. "The magic doesn't work that way. It requires sacrifice." His tone implied more—*what could you give that was more valued than your life, your safety?*

Nim sat silently for a moment then held out her hand, turning it palm up to reveal the delicate skin of her wrist, offering blood.

Warrick shook his head. "It isn't that easy. It isn't about blood. It's about sacrifice." And if she was willing to give it, blood was no sacrifice at all.

There was nothing she had of worth that she was willing to give. Allister and Margery were all Nim could claim, and even they were not truly hers. They had been stolen like everything else, belongings of previous marks—men who had been taken by the Trust. "Nothing else matters to me," she admitted. "I only want my life back." Nim sighed. She'd given her freedom twice, once for her father's contract with the Trust and again for her bargain with Warrick, which she'd hoped might help her find a way free. "There has to be another way." She could not imagine returning to the Trust without protection, without some hope.

Warrick's fingertip danced over the pad of his thumb. "Magic is paid in desire, and the bill is always a trade, a forfeit of great value." His eyes met hers. "The trouble is, the opposite of what you desire is precisely what you do not desire. Magic cannot be given freely, and the cost is as steep as its reward."

Nim had never experienced magic that was not entirely foul in the end. But his words held truth, because hadn't what he said come true? The bettor's desires were almost always mirrored into their worst fears, the things they wanted most of all taken from them by their bargain.

Warrick leaned forward, dropping his knee as he pressed his palm to the floor between himself and the chair. A strange warmth rose through Nim, the dampness in her hem chased from the material as the sensation raced over her flesh in something that was far different from the magic of the Trust. It was less slithering, less smothering, and more like a welcome hearth or the sun on her skin. Like the way his hands had felt against the bare skin of her ankles.

She jerked back to alertness, realizing at once that she'd relaxed into the chair and closed her eyes as she settled into the magic's warmth—Warrick's warmth. "Don't do that," she said. "Don't sneak up on me with—just... don't."

His expression did not change, but Nim felt her own shift. After all, she had just offered the man her bare wrist with the suggestion that he take her blood. She had pleaded with him to use magic on her. "I'm sorry," she said. "I just... I don't like it. I don't like being caught unaware."

She did not sense judgment from Warrick, only curiosity. She kept forgetting she was in his rooms, that she'd invaded his private space as a thief and, worse, as an agent of the Trust. She was committing treason. She felt sick at herself, at her situation. Calum had nearly gotten her hanged by the king, and the seneschal of Inara was on the floor at Nim's feet.

"How did you know where the coin was?" she asked.

Warrick's demeanor lost its inquisitiveness. "I can't answer that without putting you at further risk. This has already gone too far."

"But you know someone on the inside."

"If you had any idea..." He released a long breath. "Don't attempt to discover my secrets, my lady. It will only bring you regret."

"Nim."

His gaze shot back to hers.

Oh, for all things sacred. Margery was right. Nim was going to collect him like a pet. She cleared her throat. "Or Nimona, whichever you like. No sense in standing on decorum now that I've pilfered your private rooms." The sensation that came over

Nim at his reaction was so unsettling that she refused to look at it, reaching hastily for another question instead. "Why don't you wear a sword? I saw you had one in the chest of drawers."

Warrick's mouth opened is if to answer, but he shut it again for a moment as he looked at her.

Her mood was swinging like a pendulum, she supposed, but she couldn't quite help it. The evening had been a series of shocks.

"Wesley," he said truthfully. "He cannot bear to be near them. I leave my official weapon at the door."

Nim's brow rose before understanding dawned. "That was the toll on him? Not being able to be near a blade?"

Warrick's gaze floated to the far wall, where a mantel lined with sculptures sat above a bare hearth. "His father wanted him to be a great swordsman. Now, the boy cannot even pick up a sword." Nim had the sense that Warrick had seen him shy away from weapons and could not stand the idea of what the magic had put Wesley through.

A shiver ran down Nim's bare arms. "How did he get free?"

Warrick shook his head and stood. "You're digging, Nim. You'll not like what you find."

A strange thrill went through her at his use of her name, nothing at all like the ice she felt from Calum. But he was right. She'd done nothing but dig since she'd received the seneschal as a task. And she'd learned more about magic and trinkets in a matter of days than she had in years on her own. "There are a great many things I don't like," she admitted.

Warrick's gaze met hers over his shoulder, and she let him have it for a very long while. But he didn't snare her with magic. Nim didn't know Warrick, yet she could not imagine him using it to hold her too tightly and choke off her air. Whatever he saw in her eyes, whatever he felt, he held within himself, because as he turned back to his desk, Nim could detect no sensations at all from him. "Wesley," he said. "Come in."

Nim startled. She'd not even heard the boy outside. He came

through the door from the sitting room, perfect in his official dress as messenger. "Nim!" he said.

Warrick shot the boy an annoyed glance, but Wesley's focus was on Nimona. She smiled, self-consciously sliding the robe to the edge of the chair to stand, her bare feet coming to rest on the warm wood floor. Wesley glanced at Warrick. The seneschal had crossed to his desk and was pressing wax onto folded parchment. Nim tucked her feet into the slippers, which, like her hem, were entirely dry, then walked to the desk to stand by the two. Warrick slid the completed letter away from his workspace while he prepared a second.

The wax was blood red in the dim light, and Nim could not seem to resist the unsettling urge to touch it. The seal was still soft, still warm, and it bit at her like the sting of a wasp. She jerked her hand back with a gasp. Warrick gave her a look. "Why did it do that?" she hissed. She drew her wounded fingertip to her mouth, touching it to her tongue the way she might a burn. Warrick's eyes tracked the motion.

She dropped her hand. "None of your other messages stung me."

"They weren't sealed like this." His eyes went back to his work. "And those that were sealed were intended for you."

Warrick dropped the second message on the edge of the desk.

Letters sealed with magic. Nim stared at them. "So the messages you said were protected..."

She didn't need her extra sense, because Warrick's gaze told her everything. They had been safe. She could have been sending her demands and secrets all along. "Why didn't you tell me?"

He straightened. "I did." His tone was flat.

His script on the parchment came back to her: *Trust that a man of my station would know well enough whether young Wesley was safe transport of any intimate messages you wish to send.* Nim watched him for a moment, and she knew there was something more.

Warrick *liked* finding her in his rooms. He had wanted her to come.

Their gazes remained locked, and Nim's cheeks went hot. "Wesley," Warrick said, "deliver these messages then escort Lady Weston to her rooms at Hearst. I'd like you to stay at the manor until morning."

Wesley stepped forward, and Warrick scooped up the letters to place them in the boy's hand. *You know what to do*, the exchange seemed to say, and Nim wondered if Wesley truly did, if the boy could sense from Warrick intimations the way she could. She had thought it was rare, but plainly, Wesley had been through something horrid in his youth. He had been touched by magic, the same as she had. It was possible he could sense it too.

And Warrick was sending the boy with her, maybe all the protection he could give. Nim wondered how, exactly, it was that Wesley was safe. Wesley had made a sacrifice, which was clear by the scars that covered his hand, but she could not help but feel that Warrick had made one of his own for the boy.

"Get her a cloak," Warrick told Wesley.

Wesley nodded, turning from the room without further reply.

Nim did not take her eyes off Warrick. He had truly bared himself to her, as promised. He had told her before, and she had not listened. His days were spent as seneschal of Inara, and there, in his rooms, his nights were spent managing personal affairs. She stood where he conducted his business—whatever he was about with the Trust.

"What do they want you to do for them?" she whispered.

"You mean as seneschal?" He shook his head. "Nim, you misunderstand." She tried to ignore the intimacy of her name on his lips, how low their voices were, or how close she found herself to him. She tried to hear what he said beneath the words, to sense the secrets he kept. He leaned closer. "They do not want me to maneuver the king for them, to complete their tasks. They want *me*."

Nim opened her mouth to ask but never found out what Warrick meant.

He straightened. "Wesley, good man." He gestured Nim toward the boy, who was coming in with a thick winter cloak in hand. "Should keep you warm," Warrick said, a hint of fondness tingling beneath his tone, as if he'd not just confessed that the Trust wanted him killed, if that was what he'd confessed at all.

Nim glanced over her shoulder at Warrick, but he had turned his face down, busying himself with quill and ink. He was done talking. Nothing else in front of the boy.

Nim straightened and managed a flimsy smile. "Thank you, Wesley. I'm ready."

CHAPTER 17

Wesley was quick about delivering his messages, and no one asked why an unknown lady trailed after him, lurking in the shadows in the dead of night. Nim supposed if the seneschal worked all day, the private messages he sent were always delivered so late, but it seemed as if no one paid him much mind at all. He was young, yes, but there among the finery and pomp, it was plain that Wesley was no simple boy. He carried himself well, and though he was thin, he would soon grow into his lanky frame and become an imposing man, should he ever be able to keep that crooked grin under control.

Nim allowed him a smile in return, and the two were quiet as they stepped from the castle, across the grounds, and into the darkened streets of Inara. The storm had left the night air heavy, but Nim kept the cloak over her shoulders. Its collar was thick with soft fur, and from its size and style, she sensed it had belonged to a younger Wesley.

When they finally arrived at the manor, Nim was hesitant to go inside not because she was afraid to show Wesley the private corridor, but because a remembered chill of seeing Calum in the dining hall skittered over her at the mere sight of the place. She hated that he had taken one more thing from her and steeled herself to go inside. "We'll use the front door," she said. "You're an agent of the king, after all."

Wesley's shoulders shifted, as if he'd just remembered his post, and he stood tall as Nim knocked on the manor's door. Alice opened it and moved her eyes slowly from a bedraggled Nim to a boy in the king's colors.

"I'm sorry, love," Nim told her. "I've lost my key." Alice's gaze narrowed just a fraction. Nim smiled. "This is Wesley, exalted attendant to the venerable seneschal of Inara, his gracious Lord Warrick, second to the king." She considered embellishing a bit for Wesley's sake, but Alice went a little pale, and Nim thought it best to quit while she was ahead. "He'll be staying the evening with us. Please treat him kindly and see that Allister shows him to a proper room."

The girl backed slowly away from the entrance, dipped in a curtsy that did not prevent her gaze from staying on Nim, and then, when Nim nodded, apparently decided that if the whole thing was a jest, it was not worth risking the slim chance it wasn't. "Of course, my lady. At once." Her green eyes regarded Wesley. "Such a dreary evening, my lord. May we offer you tea?"

"And cakes," Nim suggested.

"Yes," Wesley said gratefully. "I would be quite pleased with both. That is, if you don't mind."

"Go on," Nim told her. "I'll show him to the sitting room while he waits." Nim loosed the cloak and draped it over one arm, taking Wesley with the other arm to lead him to the sitting room, though he very well knew its location from previous visits.

"Wesley," she asked in a soft voice, "how is it that you are safe from..." Nim considered how much she might say, how much Warrick might have told him about Nim's situation, and decided on, "the dangers of the night?"

His sharp gaze shot to hers. When they entered the sitting room, Wesley turned to her. "I am protected." His eyes darted toward the corners of the room, searching, then returned. "It was part of my bargain."

Wesley was safe. Protected. Warrick had sent him because Calum and the Trust couldn't come near the boy. Something painful swelled in Nim's chest. She knew what it was: hope. She tried to quash it. "Lord Warrick arranged it?"

Nim didn't think Wesley would give her the details she needed, but his attempt at reply was cut short as Alice shot through the doorway in her haste to serve what she might not have been entirely convinced was a king's man. The girl was not very trusting overall, and Nim found it quite charming. "Thank you, Alice. I'm afraid I am overtired and will want to retire to my room, but Wesley"—she took hold of his wrist and gave it a reassuring squeeze and him a look that promised they would resume conversation on the morrow—"please feel free to take your tea and cakes where you prefer—in your rooms or here with Allister and Alice. You're welcome to treat this manor as your home." It was not truly Nim's place to offer, but she knew Elena well enough to be assured the woman would die of shame then rise again to die of dishonor should the invitation not be extended to any agent of the king while she was head of household. "You can be at ease with them. You have my word."

Wesley inclined his head toward her. "Thank you, my lady. Rest well."

Nim made her way through the empty halls of Hearst Manor, stood at the door to her room, then walked inside, leaving the lock unsecured behind her.

"MY LADY." Allister stood staring down at Nim where she slept on the chaise, fully clothed with a borrowed cloak draped over her soiled dress.

Nim squinted up at him in the early light and groaned.

"Indeed," he said. "But I suspect it will get worse."

"Worse?"

His expression was grim. "Elena has discovered there is a king's man inside the household. She's established a schedule for the morning's events, and you have less than a fair moment to be dressed for a formal breakfast in the banquet hall."

She threw an arm over her face and groaned again. "Tell me the good news, Allister."

He considered for longer than she liked, apparently struggling for a positive note. Surely, he'd heard about the previous night's dinner guest. She didn't know if Allister knew who Calum was, but certainly, all present had noticed their tense exchange and Nim's reaction. He would have known that something of import had happened, given that Nim had left and come back much later with the seneschal's messenger in tow. Allister was far from a fool, but the more she shared with him, the more she endangered his life. "The good news is that young Wesley, when confronted by the head of household about how he has thus far been treated, sent his compliments to Alice on her service and attention."

Nim dropped her arm. "That truly is good news. Elena will have to keep her on."

Allister gave a short nod. "And now you have far less time to prepare." He glanced at her disheveled gown. "I'm afraid that one is primed to retire."

"Rags," she agreed. "But save the lace and buttons to send to Margery. Tell her I burned it in offering. She always hated this one."

Allister chuckled, or she liked to pretend he had, because his chest shifted in what Nim could only assume was the act of holding it back.

She rose to sitting. "I'll have a bath and be down fashionably late, like only the highest of society."

"Very good," Allister said. "I'll inform the head of household, so that she might prepare your noose."

A laugh shook Nim's own shoulders. "Allister," she said as he approached her door. He looked back at her, gloved hand on the lever. Nim smiled. "Thank you."

He inclined his head then slid from the room.

Nim fell back on the chaise, emotions drawn and quartered, dragged in separate directions through filth and mud so that she did not know how to reach for one or another to pull herself back together. A bath, she decided, then breakfast, and the rest would come.

AFTER AN ELABORATE BREAKFAST ceremony and various overwhelmingly structured social proceedings, Nim was grateful when Wesley finally announced his regret that it was time he take leave. She hoped he didn't notice, but the boy seemed nearly as exhausted by the morning's events as Nim.

"I think I prefer watching from the edge of the room," he admitted as Nim escorted him to the door.

Nim patted his arm where it rested through hers and turned to face him. "Thank you for staying. I indeed slept well, and I appreciate all you've done."

He blushed just a shade, awkward, she thought, because he believed it his duty, not something worthy of praise. He reached into his jacket, drawing a folded parchment from within. "This one's for you," he told her. "I was supposed to wait until this morning, but with breakfast and..." He gestured vaguely at the production they'd been put through.

Nim took the note from Wesley's gloved hand, a familiar distinguished script laying out the curves of her name above the fold. "Thank you," she whispered. *Fates save me, I am whispering.* She cleared her throat and looked at Wesley. "Thank you," she repeated. "It has been so good to know you, Wesley."

His brow drew together, and she shook off the emotion, offering him a smile as best she could. She could only hope she would see him again, but it seemed she'd not much faith in the days to come. She opened the door and watched him leave, the letter warm in her hand. When he was gone, she took it with her to her rooms, closed the door behind her, and settled onto her chaise.

For Lady Nimona Weston, Hearst Manor. The wax seal did not sting her but broke beneath her finger. And there, the black strip of material from a cloak she'd left behind. She wondered if it had been a sacrifice, if it was somehow tied to the magic that kept his message safe. Worse, she wondered what it cost him each time he'd sent her a letter, what he'd had to give up to keep it secure. But Warrick was powerful, and his magic had washed over her in a wave that had made her dizzy with its strength. The small things couldn't have cost him much, surely.

She might have known more than she ever had of magic, but she still knew nearly nothing at all.

She unfolded the parchment, and a chain slid free into her hand. She rolled her wrist to examine the thin silver band resting in the center of her palm, where it was looped through the chain. It was plain but pretty, pleasing in its simplicity like a common wedding band. It reminded her of the style her mother had worn.

She'd no idea how to feel about it.

My lady,

I trust this message finds you well. It is not within my power to prevent your engagement, but I might bestow this token as what protection I am able to offer. Should the fates allow, it will help see you through.

Yours,
—W

NIM STARED at the letter for a long moment, unsure precisely what it meant. But there was a knock at her door, and she jumped, fumbling the chain and the letter before managing to conceal both neatly between her skirts and the chaise. "Yes?"

Alice's braided head popped through the door. "You've a message, my lady. A letter."

A shiver of unease ran over Nim. "Come in. Tell me what's wrong."

She crossed the room, holding out a folded parchment without mark or seal. "It's from him," she said. "The unpleasant man from dinner."

Nim went cold. "How do you know? Was he here?"

Alice shook her head. "I can feel it, my lady. It was just this letter on the stoop and a small package that held a gown. I pitched the gown into the bushes. Something about it felt wrong." Her eyes met Nim's. "Like him."

Nim took the letter from Alice, and the girl seemed grateful to see it done. "Good girl," she said. "And you're right to be cautious. Don't ever let him see," she told her. "He likes it when you're scared."

The girl nodded sagely. She must have encountered men like him before. But no one was like Calum, not truly. He was among the worst.

"Thank you, Alice. You've done well."

Nim watched as the girl left the room, hating the way the letter felt in her hand. Alice had been right—it felt wrong, unpleasant, and nothing at all like the messages from Warrick.

Drawing a steadying breath, Nim carefully opened the folded parchment.

Tonight.

A SINGLE WORD had never looked so disagreeable. Calum had said he would send her the details, but he'd only wanted her to know that he was aware of Nim's visits from the messenger. In years, he'd never come to her home, never delivered a gown or a letter. When she'd been summoned, it had been nothing of the sort. *I see what you're about*, it all seemed to say. There was no way to know what else he had seen.

Nim stood to cross the room, threw the parchment into the hearth, then lit it with a taper from atop the mantel. She watched it burn, waited until it was nothing but ash, then stomped the ash into dust.

CHAPTER 18

W hen evening fell, Nim walked through the gates to the undercity, dressed not in a gown but the trim jacket and pants she wore for the nighttime jaunts the Trust put her up to. The collar of her shirt was high and close fitting, and beneath it, she wore the thin metal chain she'd received in the letter from Warrick. Against her chest lay a ring she prayed would offer protection.

Calum might have held Nim's contract, but he'd gone too far in sending the gown. She would not don a costume for him like a puppet whose strings could be pulled. He'd taken her from society, and she would not pretend otherwise, even while he made her dance.

The guards at the gate paid her no notice as she strode past without a cloak, baring her weapons. Her mace and dagger were not permitted near Calum, as she was held under contract, but tonight, she was his guest. Tonight, the rules were different.

Still, she could not use them to kill, only to show her teeth and remind Calum who she was. Nimona Weston would not walk easily into his games. She could not be bought by misleading promises, trapped like so many who had come before her. She would not go willingly.

"Lady Weston?"

The voice startled Nim to the extent that she missed her stride and visibly stumbled. The sentry who'd stopped her did not react but waited for Nim to gather her wits. "Yes." she said. "Why?"

She well knew why. Calum had sent the man to lead her to whatever pit of unseemliness he had planned for their evening. The sentry turned, and Nim followed, her jaw tight as she considered that her keeper had already started his games.

They made their way through several corridors, winding farther and deeper beneath Inara. Nim felt the magic drawing her, teasing at the edge of her consciousness and tugging at her attention. The undercity became more overwhelming the farther down one went, and she could not help but think of how it must weigh on her father within his cell, deeper still, near the heart of the Trust and its queen in her lair.

She shoved the thoughts away. Nim had learned her lesson and had seen others learn it too. Thinking of her father would only draw her to him, snare her in the magic that bound them, and drown her beneath its hold. Besides, the man she knew was gone. He would have been no more than an empty shell.

Instead, she watched the doorways, counting the turns and markers should she need to quickly find her way out. As they walked farther, the ceiling rose higher—or, she supposed, the floor fell lower while the ceiling remained. Long draperies hung from its beams well overhead did little to dampen the echo of sound. She kept her chin up and her face forward, allowing only her gaze to stray from the path before her. A wide door revealed a room of revelers lounging about while a man in the center was strung up by thin metal cords. Nim drew a steadying breath and followed the sentry, reminding herself of the alternative and that her lie at Hearst Manor had been the only way to keep her friends safe.

They came to a pair of doors with three serpents carved into the dark wood, their bodies tangled, their eyes inlaid with jewels

—one onyx, one sapphire, and one whose gemstone eyes had been plucked from their sockets. It called her to touch it, but Nim kept her fingers tightly in her palms. The sentry opened the door, stepped out of Nim's path, and said not a word as she came past him into the room.

Her chest constricted when the door closed behind her, leaving her alone in what she was starting to fear were Calum's personal, private rooms. Lavish furniture sat in clusters throughout the room—a wide couch near two low tables, a group of chairs upholstered in deep red, and floor cushions near a massive hearth, which was lit with a fire that did not smoke or snap. Candles lined the long table near the entrance, and sculpted iron candelabra hung from a ceiling made of stone and arching wood beams.

Magic seemed to pulse through the space like a breath, like a living, creeping thing.

"Lady Weston."

Calum's voice startled her, but Nim did not jump. She had expected him, wary that he might appear suddenly too close with his smothering magic.

Instead, he came through a far door and sauntered toward her at a leisurely pace. His tone slithered over her awareness, revealing that he was not feeling as playful as he appeared to be.

"Calum." One word, a warning to keep his distance, a promise that she intended to hold him to what propriety she could, a reminder that she was there because he'd forced her hand.

A slow smile spread over his lips. "Who else?"

Fires ignited in the stone constructs near Calum, and as he walked, a thin strip of flame followed their path in the trench around the edges of the room. It was warm, bright, and utterly terrifying, but not at all the worst Nim expected to see. "May I offer you a drink, my lady?" he said as he came to stand far too near.

Nim shook her head, her mouth too dry to speak. If she

regretted anything, it was coming there, and yet she could not have abided anything else. She kept her gaze averted, avoiding his eyes.

"Hmm," Calum said. "This coldness will put a damper on the evening." His lips twitched. "Where is your curiosity now, Miss Weston?"

"Why did you bring me to your rooms?" There was only one reason Nim could think of, and she did not like it at all. He had sent her a message, and he had brought her to his private rooms, things he had never done—things she had done with Warrick.

He slid a hand over the buttons of his vest, leaving his palm against the center of his chest. "To show you around, of course. It is, after all, your curiosity we are here to sate, is it not?" *Douse* was more like what Nim expected, had she any curiosity at all. He stepped closer, forcing her to move back and turn his direction to walk beside him. "Come now. Let's begin."

Calum led her through his rooms, lavish and excessive, and Nim could not help but be reminded of the only other place she'd been that had held such attention to detail, such riches and grandeur. But there was nothing of royalty and structure in Calum's tastes, and he seemed so far removed from the style of Warrick's private rooms that she found herself unable to not compare. Maybe Calum cared about nothing inside his rooms, like Warrick in his study, but the man had certainly not been spare about it.

She sensed something like curiosity coming from Calum and wondered if that was why he'd been so intent on accusing her of hiding her interest. "What is it?" she asked. "Are you waiting to see whether I'm impressed?"

His teeth bit at the edges of a grin. "I know it's impressive, Miss Weston." His tone implied that he enjoyed how much she picked up from him, that he knew her secret, and that he wanted to play with her talent further. But surely, Nim had not been the only one touched by magic with whom Calum had come into contact. She couldn't have been the only one to play his games.

It only seemed that he had more fun with her, for some reason Nim could not quite make out. "I've seen the hovel we've got you in at that varlet's manor. What was his name again?" Calum tapped a finger to his lips, constantly working to bring Nim's gaze to his own. To trap her.

"Hearst," she said. "You know it well."

He chuckled. "Ah, yes. What a sport that was. The man gave quite a chase." He was baiting her again, and Nim ignored it. Calum leaned against a table, plucking a grape from a tabletop bowl and bringing it to his lips.

Nim stared at the wall. "It's not a hovel. You know that too."

As if he could tell her attention was still on him, he was painfully slow to eat the grape. She did not like his teeth or anything to do with his mouth, his hands, or his entire horrid being. Nim had to fight the urge to move away, to flee his rooms and let him punish her later.

Calum slid the bowl of fruit toward her. "But now, you've seen nicer things. Surely, you can imagine something preferable to a stolen manor."

Nim's gaze nearly flicked to his, and she had to stay her emotions. It felt as if he was not speaking of his own rooms but something else—as if teasing out what she thought of Warrick's. She didn't know if she was being suspicious or if Calum truly wondered what her impression was of the man he'd set as her mark.

"Just ask your question. I didn't come here for games."

"Oh, but you did." He leaned closer, his words whispering over her skin, tightening around her and restricting her ability to breathe. Beside her, Calum wet his lips. "You've simply no idea that you're not a player." He shifted, coming near enough that she could feel the pulse of his magic in the beat of her heart. "You, my dear Nim, are a pawn."

CHAPTER 19

Calum's body was nearly pressed to Nim's, his magic pulsing through the space between them in unbearable waves. There was something in his words that spoke the truth, but more that Nim could not make out. He was hiding something, and it felt like a secret that said Nim was more than a pawn. It said Calum didn't like being played. She shook her head, trying to dispel his effect on her, but Calum kept her trapped. His fingers slid toward the high collar of her blouse.

He brushed a loose strand of hair away from her skin. "Tell me, Nimona, if you're so fond of necklaces, why is it that you don't wear mine?"

Nim's heart raced, surely betraying any outward calm she managed to possess. She had to still her hands to keep from reaching for her collar, but the ring was safely pressed against her chest. She could feel it, knew it was hidden beneath layers of cloth. Somehow, Calum knew it too.

"Was it a gift? Or a bargain? Were you so eager to trade with a man you barely know?" *When you won't bargain with me.*

"Step away from me," Nim said through gritted teeth. "You know I can't think when you're so near."

She could hear the smile in his voice. "That's exactly why I'm here. Tell me, Miss Weston. No lies, no need to think through your options. Just tell me of the seneschal of Inara."

"I can't—I don't know what you want."

A low hum rumbled through Calum's chest, as if he was deciding what it was that he wanted. He was so angry, the magic roiling in him the way it had with Warrick when he'd discovered the locket she'd brought him was a gift. Maybe that was why Calum was close—maybe gifts meant something she didn't understand. She couldn't concentrate and didn't know how to answer, but she opened her mouth to deny it was given freely, to say that she'd bargained with Warrick for the ring. Except Calum didn't want that, either, because she'd never bargained with him. Her head was pounding, her pulse hammering through.

"Tell me," Calum whispered. "Tell me of this necklace, how it came about."

"I didn't—he was angry. Angry you came to the manor and searched me out." The pressure around Nim eased, and she was immediately sick that she'd spoken at all. She pressed a fist hard into her stomach, wanting to quell the nausea and guilt. Calum knew Warrick had given her the necklace. It was supposed to protect her. And Calum had used it as an excuse to torment her. She prayed the words could bring Warrick no harm. Speaking of him at all felt like such a mistake, like a betrayal.

But Warrick was her mark. Calum knew far more about the man than he let on. The only thing he hadn't known was what had passed between them in private.

Calum straightened to back away, and Nim drew a gasping breath. "There is no need for such rules in a game well played." His words were a dismissal, and Nim had the sense they were not for her. Calum flicked his wrist in a gesture that might have been irritation, and the fires throughout the room flared brighter. "Come now," he said. "Surely, he's told you. Surely, you've noticed he's one of us."

Magic, Nim thought. *But nothing at all like Calum.* "I don't want to talk about him." She turned to face him, her eyes focused solidly on his shoulder. "I have my instructions. I'll get your watch, and then we'll be done. Whatever else you sent me there for, I'll not do it." Her fingernails cut into her fisted palms. "I'll pay my tithes, and that's all you can force me to do."

Calum dipped his head so that she could see the smile that crawled over his lips. "You know I love it when you're obstinate, Miss Weston." His tone rolled over her, saying that he did love it, because he would watch her pay for the defiance later. "Now, the night hours are wasting. Let us join the others in the revelry you were so curious about."

NIM DID NOT TAKE Calum's arm as he led her through the labyrinth of rooms and to a narrow corridor, its walls tight, closing in around them with the pressure of magic. Emotions rolled off Calum in a satisfied hum, terrifying in its constancy. Whatever they were heading toward, there was little chance Nim was going to like it.

They walked through halls that were empty of guests to a room that was a low, wide space made intimate by dim light and clusters of cushioned seating. Tendrils of incense smoke danced through the air in thin strips that seemed to want to snare Nim's gaze. Bodies draped over the furniture, languid and lovely, like a tapestry she'd seen somewhere long, long ago. A few faces turned to Calum, a few more sliding over Nim with the slithering unease that told her they possessed magic. Nothing like Calum's. None of them were the son of a queen. But there was something about them that told her they relished being near power and that they had done unspeakable things to earn their places.

Calum settled onto a chaise, forcing Nim to take the spot near him or draw further attention to herself. She perched on the edge of the seat with her booted feet flat on the floor in case she had the chance—the need—to bolt from the room. The magic was near enough that she could feel it pulse through her like a drumbeat that drew the rhythm of her heart to abandon its pace. Music echoed from one far corner of the room, laughter from another. Beside her, Calum relaxed back in his seat, the tension and curiosity he'd carried all but gone from her senses.

She took the drink she was offered but only held it cupped between her palms. She would not trust it. She would not trust anything there. Quiet conversation carried on beside them among clustered groups of something further up the hierarchy than mere accountants, more important to the Trust. Nim had never been surrounded by so many at once. It felt wrong, feverish, her body drawn to their magic while her instincts told her to run. Conflict raged inside her, but her only choice was to stay.

Calum's finger brushed along the leg of his pants, a casual gesture that Nim had never seen him make. He'd always been moving, prowling, tracking a path around her as if in hunt. His ease did nothing to relax her. Entertainment moved throughout the room, performers Nim sensed were owned by the Trust. Not all of them were magic. She stayed her gaze on the glass in her hands, even when the performers came near. Magic had a way of capturing her, and she would give it not a single chance should she be able to avoid it. Her chest, constricted by anxiety as much as Calum's nearness, swelled in a breath.

He murmured beside her, and she flinched, but his words were for someone else. His gaze trailed over Nim—she could feel it—and then he leaned forward to sit level with her. A serpent slid near Nim's boot on the floor, and she shifted both feet back toward the chaise. She wondered if there had been serpents with her father, if he had been chained to a wall, only able to hear and feel as they slithered over his flesh in the darkness of his cell.

Then she thrust the thought into its own darkness, locking it away with memories and hopes, the things that could hurt her.

"Are you enjoying our diversions, Lady Weston?" Calum's voice was muted, genuinely interested.

He glanced at her, but Nim did not look his way. "You take pleasure in hurting people." Calum could not read her thoughts, but her tone made it clear enough: she could never take joy in someone else's pain.

He smiled. "Oh, I suspect there are those who you would take a great deal of pleasure in hurting."

"I'm not falling for your traps."

Calum chuckled. "Indeed. You have always been the cleverest of my thralls. Always so difficult to bring under rein."

Nim gritted her teeth.

"I do think you'll dislike this one," he said. "Though it's a favorite among the crowd." His gaze turned toward the center of the room, where a man was brought in under mask and bonds. Nim's heart skipped in her chest, falling out of rhythm with the magic before jumping to catch up again.

It was not her father. Calum would never do such a thing. The man they'd brought in was too young, too small to be him. He was only toying with her, drawing her attention away from the safety of the glass in her hands.

She'd fallen into his trap.

He glanced back at her, the edge of his lip caught beneath his grin.

The man was released from his bonds. A dancer at the far end of the room swirled through rings of fire, and another held something dark in his hand, crimson blood weeping from his palm to seep into the velvet of his sleeve. Nim never should have looked, because she could not look away. Horrors filled every corner of the room, entertainment at the hands of men and women bought by contract. *This could be you*, the scenes seemed to say. *Miss one tithe and see what games your keeper will make you play.*

Her stomach pitched, her palms slick on her glass. A metal cage lowered from the ceiling, then the blindfolded man was tethered to its bars, his feet lifted from the ground so that they barely touched the stone tiles beneath him, to remind him he was nearly there, that if he stretched, he might just gain relief from the tension in his arms.

A figure moved behind him, someone of the Trust in a lavish red robe. Her arms moved to encircle the man, captive and blinded to his surroundings, and her fingers took to the buttons of his shirt, slowly unfastening each, one by one. When his chest was bare, she drew a fingernail down his flesh. Not playfully or teasingly, but to draw blood.

Fates save him, they were baiting a trap.

Nim's face jerked toward Calum, but he was already watching her. She remembered herself just in time, staring over his shoulder instead of into his eyes. *Watch*, he seemed to tell her. *Watch and see, because only hearing will make it worse.*

Lies. She was experienced enough to imagine what was happening when the snuffling animal sounds rose through the room. Watching would be far, far worse.

"Are you enjoying our diversions now, my lady? Or should I ask for more?"

Nim did not react to the intimations that came with Calum's words. She refused to look at the imaginings he sent her, the ideas of how he could entertain the room with a bound and blinded Nim. He had brought her there to toy with her, to draw out her fear and relish her disgust. He wanted her to see what he could do—what he would do if given the chance. She could not let him take pleasure in her torment, or it would only make him hungry for more. He was predatory, ravening, and she would stay her emotions until she was somewhere safe and alone. She had to.

"I've seen enough." Nim kept her voice low but firm.

"You've seen nothing at all," Calum told her. "But I see now that this has done little to help you understand. Come." He held a hand toward her, palm up, as if she might take it. "Let us explore another room."

Nim stared at his palm, certain that leaving with him was a mistake, but the captive man's screams ripped through the room, and a snarling, wet tearing sent a spasm through her very bones.

The glass slipped from her fingers, shattering on the floor as Calum watched.

"Ah," he murmured. "Fortunate that tonight, you are my guest."

Punishment is much nearer than you think, the words warned. *Do as you're told.* Nim swallowed the bile in her throat. She could no longer stay inside the room. In the corridor, she could get fresh air. In the corridor, she could breathe. She stood shakily, and Calum rose beside her, steadying her by the elbow. "What have you put in the drinks tonight, Phillip?" he asked a man on the next couch. There was a soft chuckle as Nim was led by, but she did not look up. She could not look again at anything in the room.

When they finally made their way through the space, their path far more steps than it had any right to be, the door was opened for them, and Calum slid a hand over the small of Nim's back to lead her through. In the hallway, she gasped as her head spun then doubled over to heave toward the floor. Nothing came up—nothing was in her stomach. Nim had expected as much. She had already learned.

Calum made a sound of disgust. "Stand up, Nimona. You've seen nothing tonight that you haven't seen before."

She wanted to stab him, to draw the dagger from the sheath at her thigh and drive it through his leg. Somewhere worse, probably, but his leg was what was currently in her view. It was a good rule, she supposed, that weapons were not permitted near him for those who were under contract.

She pushed her palms against her knees then drew herself upright. She could feel the blood drain from her cheeks and the rhythm of her heart struggling to restore to its pulse.

Calum's look seemed to ask if she was finished being so repulsive.

Nim brushed her palms over the hem of her jacket. "I want to go."

Something loathsome swam over her, and Calum turned to

walk her through the corridor. She followed at his side, neither of them speaking as they made their way through the labyrinth of turns. Nim had tried to mark her place when they'd come in, but Calum had taken her away from the room through a different doorway. She could not seem to feel her way out, up, back toward the sky and the air and her home in Inara.

Calum never glanced at her, only kept his gaze forward, his emotions within himself. He was angry, she suspected, unhappy that Nim had not played into his hands. She didn't know what he had expected. Calum had known her long enough to understand who she was, what she was capable of, and what she was not. She was never going to enjoy what he did to her or let him send his imaginings long enough that they might play out.

He opened a heavy door wide enough that they might walk through together. As it slammed behind them, every torch guttered out.

Nim gasped and stumbled not because she'd been draped in darkness but because Calum's intimations came back all at once, crashing into her in a revolting wave. A hand gripped her arm, jerking her forward through another door, she thought, into what felt like a small space where she was shoved against a wall. She tried to get free, but his grip was too much for her, and she was only pressed farther, trapped in the corner where two walls met.

Stone behind her, stone beneath her feet, Calum's breath was hot on her flesh, his thoughts slithering through her mind. He wanted to pull the dagger from her sheath, wanted to draw it down the skin of her cheek and watch the blood slide over the curve of her jaw and neck. Nim struck her head against the stone, willing the images away with pain.

It was too late to think, too late to be clever. She was trapped in a dark alcove, the pressure of Calum's magic nearly crushing her beneath its power. But the power swelled, and Nim's nausea rose again.

It was not Calum at all. He was only holding her. The magic was something else, something he wanted her to feel.

They'd gone lower than she realized, farther toward the depths of the undercity and the queen's lair. The magic always flowed and ebbed, but Nim had not felt the unfathomable power that had drawn her, allowing her to believe she was only walking through the corridors and not into another trap. There, she was snared, so it rose toward her, swelling through the room and washing over her. Her body came alive with tingling heat, her flesh on fire beneath her clothes. It wanted to burn her and devour whatever was not part of it. Whatever did not belong.

It was the queen, the head of the Trust.

It was what Calum might someday become.

His body pressed near hers, his hands still holding her against the wall. In the darkness, she felt him lean closer, sensed his face slide beside hers. "To remind you," he said, his voice a caress, so at odds with the way the magic was suppressing even her knowledge of how to breathe. "Should you be tempted," he told her. *Should you begin to believe you might someday get away.*

"I own you." Calum's whisper strung tightly around her, a physical thing. A promise that she could never be free.

CHAPTER 20

C alum was right. There was no way she could ever truly escape him. As if he could sense that she finally understood, he shoved off of her, leaving her alone in the darkness under the crushing weight of the Trust's magic.

She wasn't certain how she'd gotten there, grown so entangled with Calum, or become his favored prey. She crumpled to the floor, her palms meeting cool stone, her chest heaving in shallow breaths. Warrick's words came back to her. She was a thief in training, he'd said. A lady meant to spoil the seneschal of Inara.

Everything Warrick had told her was true. Calum had trained her and led her to Warrick like his puppet. She was a fool. She'd done everything he wanted—all he'd had to do was dangle freedom in front of her on a string holding a key and the promise of hope.

When the time came to pay her tithe, the Trust would come for Warrick, the same as they'd done to the other marks once Nimona had moved on.

Warrick would be killed or thrown into a cell beneath the kingdom he once ran. The seneschal would be gone, only the king left to write the laws and—and what, Nim didn't know.

Maybe the Trust only meant to stop the hangings. Or maybe they meant to maneuver someone into the position of seneschal who would allow magic to rise above ground and spread through the kingdom.

The thought made Nim sick, and she pushed to her knees, but she refused to die heaving on an undercity floor. She crawled forward, feeling for a doorway or any hint of escape. She found the thick wood of a door frame and followed it to the lever, though she had to stop several times as the magic washed over her in heavy waves. The door fell open into another corridor, bright with torches and entirely ordinary.

It felt like an eternity before she pulled her body through the opening then rolled onto her back to stare at the ceiling as she sucked in breath. Two men in robes strode past her, one glancing down at her with distaste. *Filthy Inaran*, he seemed to say.

Fates take him, but she didn't even care. Eventually, Nim rolled onto her stomach and made it to her feet. She was not certain which way was out, so she chose the direction from which the two men had come. It was the correct choice, and she thanked the fates when she finally stumbled into the main corridor, even though its torches were dim with the lull in magic. Dawn had come, and in the light, the undercity slept. In the light, Nim would find her way home.

CHAPTER 21

Allister found Nim on the steps of the manor and carried her to bed. He gave her a tonic, helped her into a shift, and, she suspected, burned the clothes she'd worn to crawl through the Trust into the hearth. He tried to console her, but Elena was on about another guest. It was only Wesley, Allister assured Nim, and she tried to make herself remember that she would need to show the boy the secret corridor to her rooms.

Later, after what rest she could manage and two long baths, Nim opened the door to her wardrobe to stare at the yards of fabric sewn into a dozen fit-for-society gowns. She dropped the thin blanket that wrapped her shoulders and drew out a gown at random, something dark and soft that felt heavy beneath her clumsy fingers. The sleeves were close fitting from wrist to shoulder, and the collar dipped to reveal the ring that still rested over her sternum. Alice came in with their dinner and stayed long after to tie Nim's hair into braids.

She felt untethered. But soon, Nim became aware of a draw, an itch to return to the one place it would have been best to avoid. When the niggling grew into desire, Nim squeezed Alice's hand and bid her to go. Beneath her dress, Nim laced a dagger to her thigh and outside it, the mace at her waist. She slid her bare feet into slippers that were far too slight for a walk through the kingdom. They did not slow her step.

The city seemed quiet, too settled and still, but she had no means to focus on it.

Nim came to the corridor that led to Warrick's rooms just as the moon stole free of the clouds, limning the castle in a silver glow. She glanced upward, over endless windows, corbels, and balconies, stone carved with vining roses and symbols of swords, to find the darkened glass she'd seen so many times from within. She did not know if Warrick would be in his rooms, only that she felt safer there than in her own home.

Calum would not come to the castle. No matter what else, of that much, Nim was certain.

Nim stared down at her hand on the panel of the hidden door, knowing full well it was not the threat of Calum that had led her there. She was a fool, and she knew it, but she opened the door.

WARRICK WAS WAITING FOR HER. He stood in the center of the room, facing the corridor she'd just come through. His shirt was rumpled, an ink stain on his sleeve. His eyes were uncommonly dark in the moonlight that stretched across the room.

"He's playing games with you," Nim warned before she took another step. "Calum. He-He's going to use me to draw you out, to—"

Warrick crossed to her. "I know."

She stared up at him, her eyes dancing between his. Warrick had not held her with his gaze, even that first night, when he'd caught her going through his desk. He had never taken her will. His hand had wrapped about her wrist, but her mind had remained free.

Warrick had known all of it. Everything. Right from the start.

"Why didn't you just kill me?" she said. "Why not turn me over to the king?"

I'm not a murderer, he seemed to want to say, but Warrick had promised her that he wouldn't lie. Even if the king demanded the laws, they were carried out under Warrick's hand. Every person who had been hanged for association with the Trust, with those who held magic, had been hanged by Warrick. And all the while, he had held magic too. *He's one of us*, Calum had said.

Warrick moved closer, and Nim realized with horror that she'd started to cry. It was mortifying, and she couldn't seem to stop. Suddenly, she was in his arms. All things sacred, the seneschal of Inara was consoling her. *Hugging* her.

It was a nightmare come to life. The fates were the worst, and she'd half a mind to tell them so, right there in Warrick's private study. But his arms were soft around her, warm and careful and entirely too supportive. She sagged into him, pressing her face to his shoulder to bury the tears. "Smelling salts," she muttered.

Warrick drew back to look at her. Nim shook her head. Allister would know what to do. But he wasn't there. A seneschal of Inara would only think her mad. She just needed one good shock to get her head straight.

And there was Warrick, so close and warm, his breath teasing over her skin, his very presence drawing her in. He was so strong and tender, and fates take her, but he smelled so good she wanted to taste him. Her gaze fell to his lips, betraying her completely in the one way that might make the entire episode worse.

"I need you to do one more thing for me," he said.

Nim nodded, her agreement unthinking. Whatever he wanted could do no harm, not when she could no longer believe that either of them had a chance to break free. Not even a man of Warrick's station was able to untie himself from the Trust.

But, she supposed, his position was one of the worst. All they would have to do was tell the king, and Warrick would be hanged, seneschal or not. A man of Warrick's station could not be suffered to live after such an offense. Except that wasn't what Calum wanted.

They want me, Warrick had said. Calum wanted to do the tormenting himself. Calum wanted Warrick dead. Nim had never been surer of anything in her life.

"I need you to go back." His tone said he wouldn't have asked it of her if it wasn't important or if he did not need it so badly. It did not say what it was that he needed, though.

Nim felt a little sick.

"What is it?" Warrick asked.

She shook her head. "He was... a bit angry." A strange sensation rolled through Nim, though Warrick's arms remained steady around her. "He knew about the necklace," she explained. "He didn't like it." She swallowed, the entire idea that she was wearing Warrick's token somehow different while standing in his embrace. "Didn't like that I wore yours when I would not wear the gift from him."

Warrick's eyes flashed. "As if you'd don a locket with a woman you do not even know inside."

Nim stared at him. He seemed to realize she'd fallen still and silent. He appeared to wonder what he had said, but his emotions were suddenly out of reach. Nim's voice was cool, detached. "I never told you what was in the locket." She had watched Warrick destroy it. He'd never looked at the portrait inside.

His emotions closed from her completely, and Nim backed slowly from his embrace. Nim was a pawn, Calum had said, which left only one other player for his game. "You risked what he might do to me," she said. "You put me in a position to be ..." She pressed down the revolting images that wanted to rise up and drown her. "All for a game, for some sick——" Warrick moved toward her, and she shot a finger out. "Don't," she said. "You knew what he was like, and you let me go there. You let me believe there might be some way out." She clutched her stomach with her other hand, pressing hard against the tremors that wanted to rock her, that wanted her to relive what had happened.

Warrick seemed to become slowly aware of her response and what it meant. "He hurt you."

A fluttering sort of weightlessness swelled over Nim, and she could not place the sensation. Something like falling, she thought, like being shoved off a balcony into the cold night air.

His gaze roamed over her, searching as if Calum's torment had left exposed wounds on her body. "What did he do?"

Her jaw clenched. "Nothing. He didn't touch me." She hated that he was making her say it, hated that she felt so weak. She had seen what Calum could do to a man. She knew the blood and the pain all too well. Worse, she'd seen what he wanted to do to her. But he'd done none of that. He'd hurt her without even breaking a sweat. "He only wanted to scare me. To leave threats so I might take them seriously enough to behave."

Warrick watched her for a long moment, as if assessing whether she told the truth.

She thrust her arms forward. "Look at me. Not a scratch."

Warrick did look, even though Nim's arms were covered from wrist to neck by the sleeves of her stolen dress. Then his gaze landed on the low split collar of her gown and lingered where the ring he'd given her lay against her skin.

"Tell me," she said.

Warrick's mouth turned down in something of a grimace, but Nim could feel that he would tell the truth. It was all she had. It felt like nothing. "He thought the locket could draw me in."

"No," she said, "he gave me that locket ages ago. It's been hidden outside. I've—" Her words fell off at Warrick's utter lack of reaction.

An embarrassingly long time passed before Nim realized what he was saying. Calum had not wanted Nim to steal the drum watch. *A lady meant to spoil the seneschal of Inara.*

Calum had wanted to bring Warrick a token, something he

could not personally deliver to his rooms. "He used me to sneak it in," she said. "So he knew—" She had no idea what he knew—certainly that Nim would be caught, but there had been no guarantee it would not have been by a guard.

Calum, she supposed, didn't care if Nim was hanged for sneaking through the castle. "But how did he know—" With a lump in her throat, her gaze found Warrick's. "How did he know what you would do?"

Warrick's jaw flexed.

She pressed her fist harder against the swimming dread in her stomach. "How well does he know you?"

The response that swelled over her was as conflicted as anything she'd felt from Warrick. *Stop digging*, he'd told her before. *You won't like what you find.* But if Calum knew Warrick at all, he knew Nim far, far better. He had played her from the start. He had trained her to gain entrance to a seneschal's rooms. He had known if she was given the choice, Nim would do whatever it took to get free.

She sat heavily on the floor, oblivious to the notion of finding a suitable piece of furniture. She settled into the place that being in the presence of overwhelming magic usually took her, the faraway respite from the waves of emotion and dread. It normally came on much faster. She hadn't been thinking, or she should have been home in her bed. But Nim did not always remember to make herself safe. She did not always have time. Once, she had spent hours propped against the wall of a darkened alley, and once, she'd lain on the narrow floor of the hidden corridor to her rooms for so long that Allister had had to drag her the rest of the way home. Distantly, Warrick's concern washed over her in a sensation of warning that someone was coming, that he needed her to leave.

He paced in front of her, but Nim only breathed, staring past him to a hazy wall she wasn't even certain was real. He knelt down in front of her, his massive form blocking her view. He muttered something then pinched her arm. *Well, that was just mean*, she thought absently. Then he hauled her to her feet. *You have to go*, he seemed to want to scream at her. *You cannot stay.*

He bit his lip, worrying it beneath an incisor, and Nim could not take her eyes away. There was something she meant to realize, some recognition just out of reach. But his intimations were flooding out the ability to gather the thought. She sensed when he realized he was out of time, that he had to do something to snap her out of the fog.

His eyes fell to her lips and stayed there too long and with too much intensity. He uttered a curse. And then the seneschal of Inara and second to the king grabbed hold of Nim's face, pressed his palms to either cheek, and drew her toward him.

He meant to kiss her. Hard. She could feel it from him, and...

She jerked to alertness and smacked him in the face only to yank her hand back. She hadn't meant to do it—she'd only reacted to the intimations she'd felt from him. She'd acted on instinct. She wasn't a lady anymore, not truly, but she'd been taught to protect herself. She had learned not to let anyone near.

Her hand felt hot. It was definitely a crime to strike an agent of the king, lady or not.

Warrick straightened but did not back away. He was so close, staring at her. She realized her fingertips were pressed to her lips and tried to drop them but couldn't seem to pull her hand away. He had just tried to *kiss* her. On the mouth. Where else he might have, she didn't know, but it seemed an important distinction, especially with him standing so close, watching her.

Warrick's emotions were strange, and Nim couldn't make them out. But beneath them simmered a hint of fear—not of her, she thought, but something else, a thing that might happen. His mouth formed a hard line. "If you need smelling salts, you should carry them on your person."

Nim blinked and stared a bit more.

"You need to go," he said. "I'm about to be summoned, and

you cannot be caught in my rooms." *If you're caught, they will kill you*, he'd warned her before.

He reached into his shirt and withdrew a letter. When she didn't react, he took hold of her hand and placed the parchment against her palm. "Go," he told her. "Please."

CHAPTER 22

Nimona Weston had had a fair share of shocks in her life, but none of those had involved hard kisses or agents of the king. To be certain, she'd thought of the same only moments before, but not with the determination she'd felt from him. She tried to remember that he had only been trying to snap her out of the magical haze, that he'd needed her away from his room before he was caught with a woman—an agent of the Trust— inside. Because surely, impending death should have meant something to Nim.

She shook her head, hurrying back to the manor in the muggy night air. She crossed the square, passing under a monument to Stewart's father, decidedly not taking notice of the platform used for hanging day. The banners hung limply, the atmosphere too still and sticky for their usual crack and whip. Very few loitered in the streets at night in Inara not because they might be mugged or robbed but because the kingdom was watched. Late-night activities drew attention from those responsible for keeping the Trust at bay. Because at night, the Trust prowled for takers in their game of blood debts, contracts, and bargains for favors that kept their magic fed.

Drawing her cloak tighter around her, Nim sped her step.

Soon, she was inside Hearst Manor, shucking her slippers and cloak and lighting more candles with the taper Allister had left her. Thoughts were swimming through her, worst of all that Calum had meant to use her to *spoil* a king's man. Nim had been through it all before. She understood the best thing she could do when she became attached to someone was sever the connection. Run away and never look back. It was what she would do for Margery, to keep her safe.

It was what Warrick should do to her.

Besides, he was the seneschal. If he did anything, it would be to see her hanged. She opened the letter he had pressed into her hand.

Nim,

I ask of you one final task, and with it, that you consider our bargain reconciled.

Yours,
 —W

BENEATH HIS GRACEFUL W were instructions to find a document and a strange curving symbol that Nim could barely make out. He needed her to return to the Trust, and worse, to steal from beneath Calum's nose.

She sat hard on her chaise, skirts and missive fluttering with the drop. "Fates save me," she muttered. Because as far as Nim could tell, nothing else would.

CHAPTER 23

Nim woke with the dawn not because she felt rested but because a rapid pounding echoed through her bedroom door. She sat up in a mass of tangled blankets, bleary eyed and hair askew, listening to the muffled argument on the other side. "Alice?"

The door burst open to reveal a tall woman in cloak and hood, with a small braid-haired creature with what had to have been too many limbs wrapped about her form, apparently attempting to remove the woman bodily from the hall. "Margery?"

Margery managed to draw a hand free of the tangle to shove down the hood of her cloak. "Of course it's me. Call this wretched beast off already."

Nim stifled a hysterical sound, though she wasn't sure whether it was meant to be a laugh or sob.

Alice righted herself enough to find Nim, her look seeming to ask if she wanted the woman taken down.

"It's all right," Nim told her. "Margery is my oldest friend."

Alice's eyes narrowed for a moment, so Nim directed her gaze to Margery. "I expect you owe the girl an apology, friend.

She does quite well to keep my guests from throwing themselves in unannounced."

Margery sighed. "If she would just listen to me. I told her I had no time to wait." She glanced down at the girl, who'd yet to release the hold her skinny arms had around Margery's waist. "I'm sorry," Margery promised. "I can see now that you are among the best, most loyal sort, and I can only hope someday to make amends. For now, I've nothing more to offer than that assurance and that your mistress can attest to my good name."

Alice's mouth remained a thin line, but she unlatched her grip and slid herself free. She turned toward Nim. "Shall I bring tea, my lady?"

Nim smiled. "I would be most grateful. Thank you dearly."

She curtsied then spun, and Margery watched her go. Shaking her head, Margery turned back to the room, stomped inside, and shut the door firmly behind her. By the time Nim crawled out of bed, Margery was across the room, posted in a threatening posture with her hands braced to her hips. "How could you not tell me?"

Nim's steps froze.

"I can't believe it," Margery said. "After all this time." She yanked the clasp of her cloak free, tossed the garment to the floor, then thrust a folded parchment toward Nim.

Nim stared at the letter, a cold fear settling into her gut. Warrick had promised to watch after Margery, to keep her safe. He had made no assurances that their friendship would stay intact. And doubtlessly, the truth of what Nim had done would sever their ties in the most efficient way possible. But he surely wouldn't have told her.

That left only one other person who would have, one who'd recently been writing messages to Nim and cared not for protecting her friends but only for his desire to punish her.

The letter waited in Margery's hand while Nim forced her steps forward, fingers trembling as she touched a missive she knew would be her undoing. She did not know precisely which secrets it revealed, only that Margery had come to Hearst Manor, a place she'd been strictly forbidden to visit more than once a season, and had burst into Nimona's private room.

It was for the best. Nim should have broken contact with Margery long ago. It was selfish to keep her and horrible to have ever let her believe Nim was her friend. *I'm sorry*, she wanted to cry, but she could do no such thing. Their relationship needed to be over. Nim had to let Margery go, no matter that it felt like ripping herself to pieces.

"You're not even going to open it," Margery hissed. Her elegant fingers remained balled into fists, knuckles pale where they jammed against the waist of her fine gown. "I crossed half a kingdom to get here and you're not even going to read that filthy—"

"It's barely a section of the kingdom."

Margery's eyes narrowed dangerously. She took a slow step forward. "If you think, for one instant, I'm going to let you turn cold and scare me off..."

Nim did think that, though she couldn't say why, because Margery had always cut her off. She'd always beaten Nim's attempts to end their friendship into shambles.

Her voice was low. "I may have made fool decisions more times than I care to admit, but we both know I've never been wrong about a person's character." She made the sign to ward off curses, and Nim couldn't help but think it was aimed at the last of her house staff. She'd never gotten over her single misjudgment. She took another step closer. "Despite those mistakes, I'm no fool, Nimona. And I've never been wrong about you."

Nim swallowed hard. Her words were barely a whisper, but nothing had ever felt so true. "You're wrong." She let the truth show in her gaze. "I've been nothing but a plague to you. In ways you'll never even know."

"Oh, I know," Margery said, gesturing toward the parchment. "And I can't believe I had to hear it from them."

Them. The guilt and shame Nim felt swam into something

more like dread. It had not been Warrick trying to protect her but the Trust trying to hurt her. Calum had gone after her friend.

"Do you know how insulting it was that you actually believed I fell for your stories? That I thought you needed information for business concerns?" She crossed her arms. "I've dealt with nothing but society contracts and deeds since I was a girl. I understand how they operate. I understand *that sort* of secret." She shook her head. "She'll tell me, I thought. One day, she'll be brave enough, she'll trust me enough, and then she'll come clean. I can wait."

Nim's mouth hung open, but words didn't come. It was fine, apparently, because Margery had words enough for the both of them.

"All this time. But now I see. I see why you couldn't tell me about them—ever. Because you think I'd feel betrayed by my father. By you because of how you were involved."

Margery was suddenly closer, steadying Nim by the arm before she realized she'd swayed.

"Don't you dare throw up on this gown," Margery warned. "I have a meeting at court I'm late for as we speak." She plucked the letter from Nim's hand and waved it in front of her face. "I don't know what your story is, and if you don't tell me, then I never need to know. But one thing is certain: whatever you did, they forced upon you. And I suspect my finding this out from the Trust just after you've started asking dangerous questions about a king's man means you're in more trouble than you're willing to admit."

Nim stared up at her, and her friend's rich brown eyes went soft. *What did they tell you?* Nim wanted to ask, but she was too afraid of the answer.

"How could you have told me, I decided, when you'd only come to know me in recalling my father's debt? But that's where you're wrong, Nim. Because if not for you, I might be tied to them too."

Margery knows, Nim's conscience screamed, wanting to run

from the horrible thing she had done. But Margery was not angry for that. She was staring her down, willing her to understand.

Margery was loyal. Margery had been young. She might have taken on a debt that might cost her freedom or her life and that was not hers, like Nim had.

"Did they hurt you?" Nim whispered.

Margery made a sound of disgust. "Cowards couldn't even face me. Had the message delivered through a courtier. Not even to my house. At a council meeting, for fate's sake."

Because Warrick had protected her. Warrick had kept Calum from calling on her friend.

"Are you crying?" Margery's tone fell somewhere between horror and indignance.

"No!" Nim wiped the back of her hand over her cheek. "Don't be ridiculous."

"I'm not ridiculous. You're the one weeping, when clearly I'm owed the due. Stop it. Right now."

"I'm not! I swear it. I haven't cried in years."

"I have to go to a meeting. I'm hideously late as it is. You're to pull yourself together this instant and stop this dreadful business." She leaned in to grip Nim's shoulders and give her a hearty shake. "Meet me in the morning at home. We've a plan to work out. Whatever affairs you're tied up in that involve the seneschal and the Trust, you'll make sense of with me. Before you're hanged or burned."

A strange, strangled sound rose from Nim's throat, but she swallowed it down.

"Also," Margery said, "about this Alice." Nim felt her brow draw together as her friend stood. She straightened the hem of her bodice. "I like her. Do keep her around." Then she turned and walked out of the room.

CHAPTER 24

Nim had squeezed Allister's hand far too tightly as he'd left her to her evening meal then dressed in pants and a jacket and walked through the close, hazy night air toward the Trust. *One final task*, Warrick's message had read. And then she would no longer be tied to their bargain, no longer risking being hanged on the square, should she be caught in the castle by the king's men.

She would only be tied to Calum.

Coldness settled inside her despite the heat, and she forced her feet over the cobbled stones that led to the undercity. Her instructions were clear, and she knew where to go, but the understanding of the danger she was in felt like a precise knife to her heart. A lifetime crushed beneath the weight of the Trust's magic and the slow devouring of all that she was—that was the risk Warrick had asked her to take.

It was the risk she'd been taking all along.

Her boots were silent in the massive corridor as revelers passed with no more than the occasional glance. Each had concerns of their own and desires that may not have been hers: how much value she placed on her life against her need to be free.

It had to be the right moment, her instructions had said, because Calum would be away from the Trust. Nim wondered how Warrick could be sure of such a thing, but like the Trust, the king's men had eyes in the streets of Inara. Besides, it was the night before a hanging day, only hours before men of the Trust—accountants caught settling blood debts above ground—would be strung up on a platform in the center of Inara for all to see, a warning from the king.

A couple in long red robes strode past with greasepaint smearing their faces, seemingly oblivious to anything other than their path. It was early, though, and not many revelers were traversing the corridors, so Nim lost little time to having to appear as if she were not up to the very thing she was about to do. The weight of the memory of her last visit sat heavily upon her, but Nim would not let her mind linger there. The last thing she wanted to do was to draw the attention of the simmering magic that slumbered in the depths below. Since the first time it had touched her, when she was no more than a girl, the power had lashed itself around her, and Nim had never been able to break its tethers free.

It was why she'd been drawn to Calum, why he'd been so easily able to reach her, to steal her blood and bind her to the debt her father had accrued. She'd been younger, yes, and certainly foolish, but the truth was that Nim had never been able to tell the magic no.

She was worse than the bettors because she was drawn, the same as they were, but in exchange, Nim had received nothing at all.

Laughter echoed behind her, and Nim ducked into the shadows of an unlit corridor. The undercity was a maze of passages and rooms, but Nim finally found her way to the rich corridor she'd been in only days before. The magic felt heavier there, as did her dread, but as she stared at the set of doors with three tangled serpents carved into its surface, she did not stop again to look. She only pushed it open quietly before slipping inside.

Calum's rooms were not dark, although he was gone. The magic burned in its trenches throughout the space, and the candelabra glowed overhead. As head of the Trust, Calum would have all of its power in reserve. Whatever threat he had been as the son of a queen would grow into something deadlier, something dangerous to far more than merely those under contract.

Nim hoped by the time that happened, she would be free from her bonds and gone from Inara, even if it was her only home and even if it cost her everything.

She walked carefully through the space, not touching more than she had to, and though everything inside her screamed revulsion, Nim walked through the doorway into Calum's bedchamber. She did not examine the spot where he slept, a wide space concealed by drapery and shadow, and did not look at the tapestries on his walls. She did not want to remember any of it, did not want to know. Beyond the room was another chamber, and there, her instructions had said, was where Calum kept the things he prized.

Calum apparently prized many, many things.

Shelves lined the walls of the chamber, each adorned with trinkets and sculpture, jeweled cuffs, and polished metals. Nim could not help but move closer, inspecting a necklace dripping with gemstones and gold. "I see you gave me your finest," she muttered beneath her breath as she took in a row of pendants far superior to the locket Calum had gifted her and Warrick had burned.

She followed the line of shelves to a massive cabinet that centered the far wall, her fingers itching to open its drawers. Recognizing the magic, she curled her hands into fists. It would be the worst of ideas to touch his things, when any one of them might be able to drag her to the depths below.

A shiver ran through her, and she turned toward a writing desk that appeared to have never been used for its intended purpose at all. Its surface was clean, no sign of ink or parchment, but centering the trim was the carved coil of a snake.

Nim pressed it.

A drawer slid open.

Magic swelled through the room.

She fought the urge to step back, but it was not power from Calum or an accountant. It was from the items which rested inside, which smelled of blood and sulfur and held the sense of regret. She swallowed against the emotions tearing their way up her throat and steeled her resolve. She would do this for Warrick. She would have the thing done.

And then, when nothing was left but her contract with Calum, she would find a way to sever her bonds before he became head of the Trust.

Nim reached into the drawer lined with scrolls, searching each of the seals. She'd studied the strange symbol on her message from Warrick and wanted nothing to do with any that were not his. She could only assume that once he had his contract in hand, Calum would come after Warrick full force, but Nim could not let that be her concern. She had to take care of herself.

Her fingers bumped against a small container, strangely similar to the one Warrick had in his own desk. But unlike Warrick's, the tin rattled. She stared at it for a moment, hating the desire rising inside her. She did not want to see. She did not want to touch it. And yet...

Nim cursed as her fingers slid to the tin, deftly releasing the thin latch before she was able to stop herself. Resting inside were two dark jewels, emeralds cut with a strange precision in an oddly familiar shape. Her fingertips crossed over them even as something settled low in her gut. They were the jewels from the doorway, the missing eyes from the head of the snake.

Calum's treasure. The thought was so unsettling, but Nim could not discount what she'd learned. Warrick had told her trinkets had power. When something mattered, it could be used against a person. Calum had taken a knife to the doors of his private rooms, dug the emeralds free, and kept them hidden among other valuable things that felt of magic.

Nim's hands were moving without thought, scooping up the jewels and tucking them into the pocket at her waist. Her palms grew sweaty as she fished through the remaining scrolls and finally found the one she was after. She shoved it into her jacket and closed the drawer until the coiled trigger snapped back into place.

And then, Nimona Weston, who'd done nothing but vow she would be strong and brave, turned tail to run from the room.

NIM STRODE TOWARD INARA CASTLE, a lightness in her step she wasn't sure she'd ever felt. She had made it out alive. Warrick had been right—Calum hadn't been in his rooms—and Nim had made it from the undercity intact. She had Warrick's contract, and with it, he could perhaps find his way free one day. Not only that, but Nim had stolen something of Calum's, and even if it did her no good at all, the act alone gave her a small sort of satisfaction.

She was half tempted to throw the jewels into a pit, just for spite.

She caught herself smiling as she passed a city guard and ducked her head from notice, but her mood faltered when in half a dozen strides, her gaze caught the boots of several more. She glanced up, eyes sharp, concerned by the number of king's men she'd just happened upon. Her gaze cut to a small tavern, its lights aglow, the muffled sound of a boisterous crowd within lessening her unease. Two men leaned against the front of a clothier's shop farther down, their voices low as they spoke of the day to come. Hanging day.

Crossing to the other side of the street, Nim tucked her jacket tighter to her chest. It was a fool's game to carry Trust property with so many men afoot, and doubly so when the crowds prepared to gather to hang the sort who did. She adjusted to take a less traveled route, turning down a narrow alleyway between two tall buildings and weaving toward the castle. It would be the last time she would have to risk the trip or use the hidden corridor and the last time she would see Wesley or Warrick or stand in the warm comfort of his moonlit rooms.

Nim was used to giving things up. Practice never made it any more pleasant.

A dark laugh echoed off the building behind her, and Nim's palm found the handle of the dagger at her hip. But when she glanced over her shoulder, the alley was empty. The unsettling feeling was not that she was being followed, she realized, but that she'd been drawn in a direction she'd not meant to go, pulled without her intent by the sort of dark power she'd come to expect from the Trust.

Above ground, in the streets of Inara.

Her heart paced as she stepped from the alley into the square. A king's banner snapped above her head, though the night air felt warm and still. Something crackled through the atmosphere, wanting to draw her nearer and calling her as it had always done, but more powerful, more real than before.

Icy fear spread through her, and she backed into the shadows. Her shoulder bumped the thick block of a cornerstone, and she became aware of the whisper of someone watching from the shadows with her. She jerked away from the man, a beggar huddled beneath threadbare wool, his fingers tracing a sign to ward off curses in the air before him.

Nim stepped away from the man, edging through the shadows around the square. Clouds rushed across the sky as if a storm gathered, throwing moonlight in unpredictable patterns across the stones.

The square that was otherwise empty, Nim noted. There were suddenly no figures in sight. She glanced back toward the shadows, the whispering watcher obscured by darkness. A sensation of fingers sliding over her flesh began at her shoulder and trailed down her back before spreading toward her side. She ran.

Her heart pounding, Nim shot for the safety of the castle, the secret corridor that would lead her to Warrick's rooms. She was nearly to the next alleyway when a covey of birds startled, swirling around her as they burst into flight, their wings brushing her face and tugging strands of her hair. Her steps faltered, knocking her off balance, and Nim spun to take in the square. Figures stood near the platform, men who she would swear had not been there when she'd looked only moments before.

Her feet were moving toward them without her permission. Nim was unable to stop herself until the scent hit her nose. *Cloves. Magic.*

Calum.

The thought made her stomach heave, but it was too late. She was caught in his snare, somehow crossing the distance without having meant to do so. A wave of heat dashed against the ice inside her, but Nim could not look away.

Run, something screamed deep within her, even as her feet moved closer still.

A slow smile spread over Calum's lips, and he suddenly had hold of her arm. His jacket was dark velvet, the collar studded with onyx gems. Moments before, she'd been on the other side of the square. Moments before, she'd not even seen him. She shook her head, jerking free of the fog that clouded her mind.

The scene cut through her, hot and sharp.

Castle guards faced Calum in a wide half circle, swords drawn and armor shielding their faces. Behind the guards, Trust accountants stood bound at the wrists, being prepared to be strung up for hanging day. And before them, centering the line of the king's men opposite Calum, stood a figure in the long robe and fitted coat of the highest law in the kingdom, the thin silver of a coronet gleaming in his dark hair. A longsword was sheathed at his side.

Warrick.

Nim felt herself sway, but Calum's grip held her steady. He tugged her closer to his side, his smile sliding wider as he looked to Warrick, a humorous rumble building low in his chest. "Hmm," he said against her hair, his words for the audience of a seneschal and no one else, "look what the fates have brought me." His incisor bit into his lip, and Nim looked away. "I wonder," Calum mused, "what the lady of Hearst Manor is doing out on the square so late at night."

Nim's gaze found Warrick, who knew precisely what she'd been doing out, but he seemed to be refusing to look at her. His expression was solemn, stately, and imposing, and it appeared he would not give Calum's games the dignity of a response.

As her heart struggled to regain its rhythm, so near the magic of both men and too much power, Nim realized what she had walked into—what she had been drawn to against her will and against good sense. Calum was attempting to steal his men from the gallows, from Warrick and the king.

The magic of the pilfered contract burned hotly in her jacket, and she prayed that Calum could not feel it. Fates save her, if he found the emeralds, Calum would know she'd been in his rooms.

Her knees gave. Calum jerked her hard against him.

Something hot slashed out at Nim, but it was gone in an instant. Her head swam, the magic tingling and horrid, tangling in her with desire and dread. There was something wrong with her that she wanted it, that she let herself be drawn. She knew the other voice, the one that screamed for her to run, was correct.

Calum was speaking, and Nim realized she'd lost another moment of awareness. She forced her focus to steady as Calum's words slithered down her spine. "A bargain, then, to set my men free."

"You don't care about them." Warrick's tone was cold, calm, and unsympathetic. Unrecognizable aside from the authority it carried.

"No," Calum said. "But it seems you care about her." His voice held a laugh, and Nim's heart gave a painful stutter.

She swallowed hard. Calum was bargaining with Warrick to let go of her, for each side to unhand their prisoners. And if he did not get his trade, then Calum would drag her back with him to the Trust.

"I care about the people of Inara," Warrick said. "I care about the law."

His words said Calum was breaking that law, that by holding Nim captive and interfering with the king's plans to hang those he'd sentenced, Warrick was bound to do justice in the king's name.

Calum's laugh echoed through the square, and a wind caught, snapping the banners and startling a bird from its high ledge. "The Lady Weston is not yours to care for. Lady Weston is *mine*."

His grip tightened on Nim's arm, and with it came the tightening of his magic. *I own her*, his intimation screamed, *by contract and by law,* and Nim knew, unequivocally, his next thoughts were not for her.

Warrick could sense them. Warrick would know.

Images of what Calum would do to her spilled from his mind, vivid and bloody violence of the worst kind. Slow torture, torment, and pain, as he watched all the while with his dark eyes holding her in place, her blood feeding his magic.

Nim's stomach heaved, and she doubled over, pressing her hands to her middle as Calum forced her to live through the agony without raising a single hand. All for Warrick to see. All for the threat.

It would be worse than what he was imagining, though, Nim knew. Because inside her jacket were things he would find in his harrowing—things she had stolen from the Trust. Nim's agreement would be forfeit. Nim would be his to do with as he wished.

Magic swelled through the square, hot and sulfurous. It burned Nim's nose and seized the breath inside her chest. The crushing weight of it settled over her, more powerful than any she'd felt. Her fingers curled into fists against her middle. Her dagger was within reach.

She could grip it. She could stab Calum.

He would kill her, of course. But it might have been the preferable way to go—quick, uncomplicated by torment and the slow devouring of all that she was, and away from the darkness of what waited in the depths beneath Inara.

"*Stop.*"

The voice was hard and sharp, a command laced with power beyond just a station. Warmth spread through her as Warrick took a step forward. "Take your men and go."

Nim was on her knees beside Calum, one arm wrenched up as he held her in his grip. She felt the sense of pleasure from him. Calum thought that he had won. Not the bargain, not his men. Calum had found Warrick's weakness. Calum had won something bigger.

CHAPTER 25

T he line of king's men sheathed their swords at Warrick's command, and the Trust's accountants were set free. Calum cared not at all—he never even gave them a glance. His eyes were on Warrick as he shoved Nim to the stones and pressed his cane to her back.

Do it, and I will end you myself, a silent threat seemed to whisper from Warrick, but Nim lost another moment to the pressure of their magic.

Then Calum was gone, and strong hands drew her up, careful of their grip. She was escorted from the square in silence, the usual noises of Inara seeming to have been swallowed up. In the shadows, Warrick gave a command, and the king's guard swept from the street, off to regain their lost prisoners, bodies for hanging day.

Flashes of moonlight and shadow flickered before her, then torchlight and darkness, and Nim became aware she was in Warrick's arms. He did not look down at her. His emotions remained hidden from her.

It was clear that Warrick could read Calum. She did not know if Calum could read Warrick too.

They walked in the darkness of a corridor along a route Nim

was not familiar with. When her eyes came open again, Nim and Warrick were alone in his rooms, and he was leaning over to settle her onto the plush chair where she'd sat before.

"Here," he snapped, and her eyes fluttered open to find a glass of amber liquid before her face. She drank it in one gulp then promptly choked.

She sat up, coughing. "What the deuce is that?"

Warrick knelt before her. "The closest thing to smelling salts I have."

She rubbed her chest. It seemed to be working, at any rate. Warrick was probing her arm. "What are you doing?"

He didn't answer, but the fog was beginning to lift by the burn of the drink and the heat of Warrick's power. Fates save her, he was boiling with it.

"You're angry," she said.

Green eyes bright on his task, Warrick steadfastly ignored her, keeping every emotion she might have sensed from him locked away.

Nim jerked her arm back. "I'm not hurt. I'm sorry, truly. I had no intention of... I couldn't help it. But I'm sorry you lost the Trust's men."

His gaze cut to hers, so intense that she drew deeper into the cushions of the chair. He was so angry, but not at her. She didn't need to feel it; she could see it.

"Will the guard be able to recapture them in time? Maybe the king will never know." The words felt strange and childish, but Nim couldn't seem to stop herself.

Warrick stood, looking away from her though his words had never been more direct. "Why didn't you tell me?" He ran a hand through his hair, a gesture that spoke of his unease. Then his fingers found the coronet, and he drew it free. Something slipped through his barriers, a memory of Calum promising what he meant to do.

He set the coronet on a table then carefully removed his jacket to drape it over the chair. His jaw tightened. "I know you could feel it. For all that is sacred, why did you not tell me what he intended—"

His words choked off, but Nim could still feel his disgust at Calum and at what he had wanted to do to her.

Then she sensed that Warrick had thought Calum was only using her as a pawn in his game. He hadn't known that Calum considered her anything more than a means to an end.

Sickness swelled through her, but not her own. Calum had interest in her, a desire to hurt her in ways that made Warrick disgusted, but Nim could not quite make out the rest, something that made Warrick ill, that felt of a bond or connection. Perhaps his contract.

Her face was pinched in concentration when Warrick looked up at her, and what emotions she had reached cut off at once.

"I'm tied to him," she whispered. "I will always have to go back."

His expression went hard. "I would have never asked you to go."

"It doesn't matter anymore. You have what you wanted. You'll finally be free." He could be free in the way he'd freed Wesley, she meant, but when his brow drew down, she realized it had maybe sounded as if she was promising he would be free of her as well. Their bargain was complete.

She drew the contract, only slightly worse for wear from the adventure it'd had, out of her jacket.

Warrick took it from her without a word, another undefinable emotion coming from him as his magic swelled through the room. He crushed the seal with a burst of power, a line of blood dripping over his palm. Before Nim could as much as gasp, he had a strip of material over the wound, turning to face her as he handed back the scroll. "It isn't mine."

She stared at him, wavering between shock at what he'd done and annoyance at his mood. She jerked the parchment from his grasp and stood to shake it at him in a fit of anger but fell suddenly short of words.

Something very, very strange passed over her senses. Something far away and long ago.

Nim's gaze left Warrick to trail down to her hand, where a smear of blood crossed the broken seal. The unsealed contract felt of warm ale and calloused hands, of the honeyed treats her father had brought her as a girl. It echoed words whispered at her mother's bedside, promises that it had been worth the sacrifice and that their Nim would be the one to see it through.

A lock of dark hair drifted from within, falling to the floor at her feet, hair the color of Nim's.

Mouth agape, emotions swimming, Nim stared down at the offending lock, and the parchment rolled in her palm, broken by magic. Stolen from the Trust.

It was *her* contract.

Warrick had never had her stealing for him at all. Everything he'd had her do was for her. She had stolen back her own freedom, entirely unaware. She let out a strangled sound, her eyes flying to his just as he averted his gaze.

Nim had just won her own life back, because of him.

NIM LEAPT AT WARRICK, unable to stop herself, the contract smashed in her grip. He only made it a step away before she grabbed him and jerked him toward her by the shoulders of his shirt, the uniform of a king's man.

"For all things sacred, why did you not tell me?" She shook her head. She was free. Actually free. "I can't believe it," she whispered. "I never thought, truly..." Glancing up at Warrick again, Nim's hand slid toward his face with the intention to press her palm to his tightened jaw. To thank him. But she'd tugged his shirt askew in her fervor, and her fingers grazed his bare skin where the ragged scar tracked one side of his chest.

It tingled with magic familiar to Nim in a more than unsettling way. The magic was not Warrick's.

Her gaze cut to his. Calum had caused the scars that crisscrossed his flesh. Her stomach turned, but she did not remove her hand. In her other hand, the contract—*her* contract—waited.

Warrick had saved her, even with a painful understanding of the sacrifice it might cost him.

His hand came up to wrap around her wrist, but he never took his gaze from hers. "You have to leave." *Before it's too late.*

"What do you mean?" Nim's voice was small, tremulous.

"He knows. You'll never be safe."

She shook her head. "I was never safe before. But now I'm free. I have my contract—"

Warrick stared down at her, and Nim wasn't certain whether she was more afraid that he might be saying she could fall again into Trust hands or of what she was feeling from the man before her.

"You want me to leave Inara."

His voice was low, a vow. "My waking hours are devoured by thoughts of you."

He was telling the truth. He *always* told her the truth. Warrick couldn't stop thinking of her, and she was a risk because he was unable to do otherwise. It didn't matter that he was seneschal and she'd fallen from good society. *Devoured*, he'd said. She felt a strange sort of pressure in her chest, but it wasn't magic. "You have a lot of waking hours," she whispered.

Warrick's mouth went into a hard line. "He won't let you go easily. Not when he knows he can use you." *To get to him.* Nim was the thing that might do Warrick in, the thing Calum could finally use against him. The thing he'd grown attached to.

She felt herself sway. She should have brought Allister's salts or a tonic. The last thing she needed was to lose consciousness. She didn't want Warrick to attempt to shock her out of it with a kiss again... did she?

She stared up at him. Fates save her, but she absolutely did. His look seemed to warn her not to try, but he did not remove his hand. He did not step away.

"I won't let you risk being bound to him again. He cannot lay a hand on you, or he will do his worst."

Nim stammered. "I'm—I can't just leave. I have things. I'm supposed to see Margery in the morning." She knew her excuses were weak, but she needed a moment to clear her head. To think. Plan.

"No." Warrick drew her hand from his chest. "You'll take Wesley. He can protect you from the magic. The two of you will be safe together."

The words felt as if they were more a reassurance for himself than for Nim, but she could not decipher the eddy of his emotions. "I'll"—she swallowed—"need to gather my things."

"Take nothing. Go now." *Before it's too late.*

Before Warrick found he could not let her go.

Her heart swelled painfully. Nim's thoughts swam as Warrick moved to his desk and released the latch to a hidden drawer of coins and jewels. He seemed to be rattling off the next steps in his mind, what they would need, routes they would take. It did not feel as if it was the first time he'd considered the outcome. It did not feel as if he *wanted* to let her go.

Nim stepped forward, her throat going thick. "You don't know what you've done for me. I will never be able to repay you."

He glanced back at her with a self-deprecating half smile that said it was a gift given freely from a man who held magic.

She wanted to examine the idea—their peculiar obsession with giving without exchange—but in the tilt of Warrick's head and the short flash of his teeth, a sudden, sickening recognition flickered over her.

It was the way his incisor caught at the edge of his lip.

She took an involuntary step back.

It was not just recognition but what she'd always sensed in Calum's emotions, the way he thought of Warrick. It was what she'd felt from Warrick—the regret at a connection, the bond the two men had shared. She had known there was something between Calum and Warrick.

She had not realized they were brothers.

Warrick had magic. The two men had been powerful enough to draw her to the square. Together, they were more powerful than any magic she'd felt.

For all that was sacred, Warrick's mother was head of the Trust.

The air came out of her in a rush, and Nim's knees threatened to buckle, but she locked herself in place, drawing on years of practice. It was a secret far more dangerous than a seneschal having power. The king had made his stance clear. If he had any idea the man ruling at his side, hanging in the king's name anyone who practiced magic, was the son of the queen, it would be worse than just Warrick's death. Stewart's rule would be questioned. No one would believe the man hadn't known or that he was not compromised by a magical bargain. There could be no other way he would allow it.

The king would lose support, surely. His rule would be questioned. Nim found herself questioning it as she stood.

And with dissent, fates save them all, the Trust would finally have the upper hand, and Calum would be poised to challenge for control of Inara.

Nim held very still as Warrick scratched a quill to parchment, apparently unaware of her world-altering revelation. His ties to the Trust were far more dangerous than she'd ever imagined, and standing alone in the dim light of the seneschal's room, she was suddenly terrified of a single truth: if he had any sense at all, Warrick would kill her.

He could never risk his secret being revealed. She was a liability—not just to him but to the kingdom. He'd told her not to dig. If she let on, he would have no choice but to act and destroy the danger she presented. He would be a fool to let her go.

He turned to her, parchment in hand, and Nim curled her grip around her crumpled contract.

"This document will get you past the walls, and Wesley will have what you need to do the rest." He had already given the boy instructions. He had planned it from the start. He had meant to save her, even before all the rest.

Nimona had a chance to be free.

She gave a sharp, decisive nod. She wasn't about to die for a fool thing like confession.

"Wesley," Warrick called, startling Nim as he handed over the document. "Come in."

Wesley seemed a bit disheveled and scattered, as if he'd been asleep, but the moment Warrick uttered the words "it's time," the boy's face fell into solemn determination. An understanding passed between them. "Yes, my lord."

Fates save her, they'd both known all along.

CHAPTER 26

Nim was rushed from Warrick's rooms in tow by Wesley, the contract shoved in her jacket and her pulse a drumbeat her steps could not match. Inara was her home, and she'd never truly wanted to leave, but she could not stay. There was no sense in gaining freedom only to allow it to be snatched away again—or to be used in a power struggle and end up killed by one side or the other.

She had compared Calum to Warrick so many times, and so many events had placed them both in her mind. It could not have been that she'd never noticed their resemblance but only that she could not fathom Calum as anything but horrid. And Warrick, well, he had felt like safety.

That safety was gone. The only thing that remained for Nim was to get out of Inara and leave everything behind.

Everything. An irrational fear surged through her. But no matter how she tried to shove it down, she knew it was not irrational at all. Calum would repay her, the moment he realized what she'd done. And if Nim wasn't there to receive his punishment...

Her hand squeezed Wesley's as she pulled him to a stop. They were in the dark streets of the city, barely lit by the glow of a sun threatening to rise. There was no time, and she knew it, but it would be her only chance. "I have to go to the manor, just for a moment. There's something I must do."

Wesley shook his head. "I'm under orders. I made a vow, my lady."

"Wes," she said, "we have to warn Allister. You know we can't just leave him."

"Warrick will protect him. There's not time." He tugged her hand, trying to urge her to move again. "It's not safe."

He was too honorable. He would do as he had promised despite any attempts she made to convince him otherwise. And he was right. There was no time for any of it.

She leaned toward him, forcing him off balance. "I'm sorry, Wesley." And then she jerked her hand from his and ran the other way.

It was reckless and ill-advised, but Nim could not just abandon her friends. She owed it to Allister to give him a chance to escape. And if he chose to stay, he needed to know the danger she'd put him in.

Warrick could not keep him safe forever. And Margery— Nim would have to get a message to Margery. She would have to warn them both.

She had to tell them she loved them. That she was sorry.

Wesley was fast, but he was burdened by packs and supplies. Another man might have dropped them, but he was too loyal. He would do as Warrick had commanded. He would follow their plan, and it involved the documents and supplies inside those bags. He would not deviate from his orders.

Her boots pounded silently on the cobblestone streets, taking her turn after turn to the place she'd spent years living as a lady despite being cast from society. She was a lady no more— Nim was free. As soon as they crossed beyond the walls of Inara, she would no longer be under the king's protection or the rules of society and no longer under threat from the Trust.

She turned another corner, breathless, and heard Wesley's

footfalls behind her. He would catch her if she had to slow at all. But as Hearst Manor came into view, she saw the front door was open, a stroke of luck she had not counted on.

"Nim!" Wesley shouted from behind her. "Stop!"

But her feet only drove her faster. She needed nothing from her rooms, nothing from the library. She could live without it all. She just needed them to be safe.

She burst through the entryway and fell to a stuttered stop. A tray was overturned on the tile floor, ceramic shattered to bits and the kettle on its side in a puddle of dark water. She took a step back, but Wesley came in full speed behind her, slamming into Nim with the force of his momentum. He grabbed hold of her to steady them both and did not let go.

"Nim," he whispered, nothing but dread.

Nim felt it too. Magic, hot and sulfurous, spread through the room. *Run*, it told her. *Run*.

NIM DID NOT RUN. It was far too late for escape.

Calum was inside the manor. A crash echoed from the dining hall, followed by a small whimper of pain. Nim dashed toward it, fighting hard against Wesley's grip. But the boy had clearly heard it, too, and he knew what it was to be tortured by magic.

Neither of them could let it be, even if Wesley knew he was breaking his vow and even if they both understood it was a mistake.

They crossed the entrance hall and went down the corridor, but not a single member of the house staff was in sight. As soon as they came through the doors to the dining room, Nim fell to a stop with Wesley's hand still gripping the material of her jacket. He would protect her from the touch of magic, if nothing else.

Calum sat at the head of the dining table, his chair turned toward the door, with one leg crossed loosely over a knee and Hearst's finest teacup in his hand.

In the other hand, he gripped a rope that held Alice by the neck.

"Ah, Nimona." Calum's pleasure was predatory and disturbingly genuine. Nim had been a fool for not leaving, for ever thinking she could escape. He set the cup on the edge of the table. "So good of you to come. I was afraid you might keep me waiting." His smile tipped at the edge, flashing that familiar revolting grin. "You know how I hate idle time. I was just planning distractions while I finished my tea."

Nim's gaze scanned the room. Two shapeless masses lay near the far wall. The rest of the house staff stood huddled at the other end of the room with Allister among them, front and center. His expression was grave. His eyes flicked to Elena, who stood slightly off to one side, not nearly sufficiently terrified, then back at Nim.

There was a small cry as Calum stood, his hold on Alice made possible by a short length of cord. The action forced her to rise to her knees beside him, her eyes pressed closed. Tightly as she held them, she could not hold back the tears.

"Now," Calum said as he straightened his coat, "to business."

He took a step forward, and Wesley slid beside Nim. She could feel his hand tremble against her, but the boy stood firm.

Calum's gaze remained leveled on Nimona. "You stole from me, Lady Weston." The contract was smashed beneath her jacket, and she wished she'd burned it when she had the chance. Calum's tone went deadly. "Did you think I would not feel when the magic was broken, when those bonds were released?"

Obviously, she had not known. It certainly would have kept her heading straight for the border of the kingdom.

He could not kill Nim, not by their laws or the laws of Inara, but he could cause her an unbearable amount of pain. He could hurt everyone in the room until they were begging for death, willing to sign away their freedom.

Calum seemed to sense her understanding. His gaze slid to Wesley. "Fetch the seneschal."

Wesley hesitated. He would have known that he should do no such thing, but before him was Alice at the end of a rope, her neck red and bruising, her life in the hands of a man who had proven what he was capable of time and again.

He had done the same to Wesley.

It was not a decision that Wesley could easily make. He was meant to protect Nimona alone.

"Nim?" he asked.

Nim shook her head. She could not leave. She knew what Calum would do.

"Enough," Calum said. "I'm sure you're sworn in some ridiculous manner, all honor and duty." He rolled his eyes then gestured toward Nimona. "I can't touch her, truly, with you at her side. But nothing you do from there can stop me from ripping apart this little girl right here." He gave Alice a shake, and her face closed into a pinched caricature of terror and pain. "Neither of you are willing to let that happen, so stop wasting time."

He was right. Nim could not abandon her. It was not an empty threat. Calum would not just torture Alice. He would hurt all of them in horrible, intolerable ways. But if she stayed...

"Me for them." The words came out before Nim could stop them, but Calum only shook his head.

"I don't need you any longer, Miss Weston. Not after tonight." He kept his dark eyes on Nim, his words for Wesley. "Go get him, boy. For every quarter hour he's not here, I take my due. More, should I find myself impatient. The lady Nimona stays with me." He gave a hard tug to Alice's leash, and the girl's eyes flew open, bright and green and terrifyingly certain. She had to have known she would be killed. She knew the sort of man Calum was.

Nim looked to Wesley, who wore a tortured expression, and gave him a single nod. *Save Alice. And Allister. And all the rest.*

Wesley gave a tight squeeze to her coat, but he turned to go, his packs dropping to the floor and his steps echoing swiftly through the hallway before the sound disappeared and the dining hall was quiet once more.

"Come," Calum said. "Sit."

When Nim didn't move, he shook his head as if disappointed. He ran a thumb over the rope in his hand.

"You think he'll come with an army." Calum's voice was low, only for Nim. "But he won't. He'll come alone. Our dear seneschal would never risk king's men over business with me." *His brother.* "He will give himself up for the lot of you, and you'll all be free to go." His gaze pierced her. "As long as you play nicely."

Do as I tell you, his intimation said. *Play the game. Trap him, and you'll go free.*

When she did not respond, Calum clicked his tongue. "It's a pity, really, that you cannot behave." He shoved Alice to the ground and came for Nim like a striking serpent. She turned to run but wasn't fast enough. Before she'd made it from the room, his cane cracked her ankle mid-stride, sending her sprawling over the fine marble floor.

Someone cried out from the back of the room, and Nim rolled to see Alice scrambling to her feet, launching herself at Calum from behind. He turned to knock her aside, and Nim drew her dagger, but the moment Calum's cane smacked the side of Alice's head, he spun back to strike Nim.

His blow landed true, and her dagger flew from her hand, clattering to the far side of the room as blood poured from her knuckles. She cursed. Calum looked disgusted.

Allister smashed a heavy serving dish over the back of Calum's head, and he ducked and spun, giving a solid blow to Allister's ribs that tumbled him into the chairs as Nim struggled to free her mace. Calum turned to stride forward then grabbed Nim by the hair as she readied her strike. But he was unnaturally fast, and Calum's foot came down hard on her hand, pinning it to the floor as he lifted her toward him by her hair. "Try it again, my lady, and see what punishment it earns."

It was truly a dare. Calum wanted her to fight him. He wanted to punish her, just to see Warrick's face when he arrived to find her bloody and beaten.

"You're a sick, sick man," Nim whispered. "And I have hated you since the very first."

His mouth slid into a vile grin. "That's more like it."

Then he drew back his cane and took a full swing.

CHAPTER 27

C alum had dragged Nim halfway around the dining hall by the time the sun rose. Her blood made a path through the room, coiling and tangled like the body of a snake.

The fight went out of her as she lay at Calum's feet, chest heaving with breaths that hurt more than they should have. Alice cried silently beside them, bloodied from her attempts to bite and claw at her captor. At least one of her fingernails had been torn off in the struggle, and red smeared over the cord that crossed her neck, lashing her to Calum.

"I'm sorry," Nim said. Allister had continued to fight, as well, though he'd fared far worse. Calum had no interest in toying with the rest of the staff. He did not know any held her concern in the way someone would have who was so near the age Nim had been when she'd been trapped in his hold, tied to a contract with blood he'd drawn, entirely unaware that he'd been stealing her freedom or of what it would cost her.

She coughed, tasting blood, and spat toward Calum's feet, not quite out of fight yet. He kicked her hard in the ribs, and she rolled to her side. "Get up," he said. "He's here."

Warrick. Nim did stand, not because she felt as if she could but because she refused to allow him to see that Calum had brought her so low. She stumbled and wiped a bloody hand against her hip, sorting the mess of herself as best she could. She felt Warrick before she heard him, the warmth of his magic, his anger, flooding the room.

"Stop right there," Calum warned as Warrick stepped into the entrance, a grim-faced Wesley hurrying to keep up behind him.

Warrick did not stop. He strode toward Calum, fist cocked for a blow.

Calum threw Alice between them and drew his cane high.

"No!" Nim shouted.

Warrick froze.

Everything seemed so real in the daylight, the blood too red, the girl so terribly fragile and small. Bright morning sun cast away the shadows that had always hidden parts of Warrick. Parts, Nim realized, that did not just remind her of his brother at her side.

Warrick's eyes trailed over her before he speared Calum with a glare. *I warned you*, the look said, and his words from before echoed through Nim. *Touch her, and I will end you myself.*

Nim felt Calum smile and glanced in his direction as his hand slid around the back of her neck. His gaze had gone as black as onyx, daring Warrick to act. Nim was certain had it not been for her, for Calum's fingers near her spine, Warrick would already have struck.

"I've been thinking a lot about how to hurt her," Calum said. "I've decided, to best effect, this one should go in fire." He flashed his teeth. *I know how you like fire.* Images lashed out from Calum of flames licking over Nim's skin, of long ago when Warrick had tried to stop his mother from burning the women who might bear a king's heir. Nim tried to jerk away from him, but Calum only tightened his grasp.

"Alice," Nim said, her words only for Warrick. Surely, Wesley would have told him, but Nim needed Warrick to understand.

Calum would do his worst to the girl, and Nim could not allow it.

Warrick's fingers flexed then curled into his palms, and Calum drew Nim's body in front of his. In his free hand, he coiled the cord around the girl's neck tighter. *You know what I want*, Calum's intimation said. *Surrender to my demands or watch them suffer.*

"The king's men are outside the manor." *Waiting*.

Calum laughed. "You won't involve them. I know where your loyalties lie." *Traitor*.

"And you," Warrick said. "I've noticed you've brought none of the Trust's men along."

Nim could not decipher precisely what that meant, but she felt the rage build in Calum.

"They aren't necessary," Calum snapped. He jerked Alice tighter in front of them both, and her thin shoulder pressed into Nim's side. He took a slow, deliberate breath then sent imaginings to the girl, plain for Warrick to see and worse than any Nim had sensed before. In them, Alice was shrieking and covered in blood, trapped beneath the earth where the magic was heaviest, crushed by darkness as serpents writhed over her form, blinded and alone, Calum's violent promises swimming through her head, ceaseless and vile. Alice, touched by magic, brushed by the power of a queen.

The imaginings stopped, and Calum unleashed a snap of power that wrapped around the girl in an unbearable grip.

A bone cracked.

Alice screamed.

It was the exact pitch as the one Calum had imagined, and Warrick's gaze met Nim's over the girl's braided head. Nim could feel the conflict raging in him. It seemed as if Warrick could not stop the sensations spilling forth, memories of what he had done to save Wesley—and what it had cost. She saw precisely how the deed had wrought the jagged scar across Warrick's chest in a bargain he'd made against his will.

Warrick's sacrifice had freed Wesley, wrought with his own flesh and blood, and it had nearly killed them both.

As Warrick looked at her, Nim could feel that he was torn between ripping the sacrifice from her to save the girl or letting Alice suffer. He wanted neither, but he knew which would wound Nim less. The idea of hurting her at all was repulsive, and he hated Calum for it, but Warrick could not make the sacrifice himself. It could not be given freely. And he had already gone too far in his long-ago bargain to save Wesley.

Alice meant nothing to him, not compared to Nim. But Calum's magic drove into Alice, his intimations causing her physical pain, the cord around her doing worse.

"Do it." Her voice was steady, willing him to understand before it was too late. Warrick's gaze was on Nim as he made the decision. She felt his guilt for only a moment before it hardened into resolve.

Pain tore through her, searing hot and sharp like a jagged knife drawn straight from the coals. She dropped to her knees, the force of the magic tearing her from Calum's grip, and the crack of power resounded through the room, stealing from Nim a sacrifice to save Alice.

The girl dropped to the floor, her bonds cut with the same jagged knife, and Calum's expression turned murderous. Nim knew it to be so, because somehow, she'd gone flat on her back, staring up at the man beside a collapsed little girl. Nim could not hear the girl's breath over her own panting, so she could only pray Alice was alive. Calum's magic could no longer touch her.

"Leave," Warrick said.

Calum stared at his brother. "This is Trust property."

Warrick jerked his head, and Wesley rushed forward then handed a document to Calum over the sprawled forms of Nim and Alice. Calum's eyes narrowed, but he took the parchment, his skin never brushing Wesley's in the process. The boy backed slowly away.

"Seized?" Calum was incredulous, his glare finding its target before he could possibly have finished reading the entire document.

"In the name of the king." *You know the rules*, Warrick's words seemed to say. "Citizens of Inara who associate with those who traffic in magical favors forfeit all property and lands. Hearst Manor belongs to the kingdom now."

There was a gasp from the back of the room, followed by a muffled thump. The head of household, if Nim had to guess. Served her right.

Calum hurled the document to the floor. *You can't do this.*

Warrick could. Warrick was seneschal.

Nim choked on a disbelieving laugh, entirely overwrought. Calum glared daggers at her. He shifted forward a step, but Warrick did as well.

"You're forgetting our bargain," Warrick warned.

Calum's attention was back on his brother, his response clear. *You may have stolen this property, but I own her.*

"That's where you're wrong." Warrick's hands were ready at his sides, almost eager for the man to rush him.

But Calum did not. Because Calum recalled the broken contract. He owned Nim no more.

His grip on his cane went rigid, white-knuckled with rage. Around him lay the carnage of his attack, Alice and Allister, and his favorite mouse to run through the maze.

Touch her and you're forfeit, Warrick warned.

A growl ripped from Calum, shattering glass along the dining table and rattling through Nim's bones. She curled into herself as the paintings lining the room crashed to the floor, but in a moment, the sound and fury had vanished. She wasn't certain how much time had passed, but when she opened her eyes again, Calum was gone.

Nim rolled to her side, edging nearer where Allister lay, and though he watched her, he did not attempt to get up. A long bruise shaded the side of his face, one brow swollen an angry red. They stared at each other for a long moment before Nim released a shaky sigh.

Allister's glance strayed to the torn fabric and stinging heat of her shoulder, his expression uncharacteristically unstable.

"Yes, I know," Nim said. "Slithery prig entirely ruined my favorite shirt."

It was a heartbeat, but Allister's mouth straightened into its place. "It's hideous, my lady. I've always meant to tell you." He coughed then stifled a groan. "Should have burned it straight away."

"You wound me, Allister." The corner of his mouth tightened, and Nim smiled. She would get him, one day.

Warrick's hands slid beneath Nim's knees and shoulders, and he lifted her with ease. "See to the others," he told Wesley then turned to walk from the room.

CHAPTER 28

Warrick carried Nim to her room and settled her on the chaise. She sat up, her jacket a tattered shred, her hands a bloody mess. Warrick went to the washstand then poured water from pitcher to basin. When he returned with a cloth and bowl, kneeling before her, his eyes were on his work, the crusted blood of her busted knuckle. "I ruined your plan," she said.

He made a noncommittal noise in his throat.

She sort of loved him for it. "Thank you."

His mouth turned down at the edges, but any intimations were bottled tight. Her hand felt small in his as he carefully traced the damp cloth over each of her knuckles.

"I'm supposed to meet Margery," she said. "I need to tell her, I need—"

"I had a message sent early this morning."

Nim stared at him.

"You told me she was expecting you. I took care of what affairs I was able."

She swallowed an emotion she didn't want to examine—guilt and something more fragile, too tender to acknowledge.

Warrick rinsed and wrung the cloth, finally raising his gaze to her face, but he did not look into her eyes, only trailed the cool water over her brow and cheek, down her jaw. Then he helped her from her jacket, tossing what was left of it onto the chaise beside her before he moved behind her on the seat. He drew a strand of her knotted hair from her neck, and there, he was still for a moment before moving on.

His touch grew even gentler, barely grazing her flesh as he slid the torn collar of her shirt aside, easing the tangled fabric from the thin chain he'd given her. Nim dreaded what she might feel from him once he took in the wound. No matter that he'd done the right thing—the only thing—she knew he would be ravaged by guilt. The marks stung but did not bleed, already scars as they would always be, a painful and constant reminder of the toll paid to magic. A sacrifice.

Warrick lay his forehead against her shoulder, where her neck met the bared flesh that was untouched by the wound. She felt his breath come out, felt the unleashed wave of his guilt and regret, felt the tremor of his relief that she was alive and that Calum hadn't hurt her.

His hands came to her waist, holding her, and then Warrick lifted his head to brush his lips to her skin. The gentle kiss was an apology and something else, something that felt like a promise. He was going to keep her safe. Hide her where she could not be burned like the others.

A shiver rolled over Nim at the thought, rumors she'd heard about the dark magic that had taken the king's secret wives before they could produce heirs. Warrick had seen it. Warrick wanted no part of the fire.

"I'm not going to run," she said. It was clear she could never be free, not while Calum was alive. Not while the Trust could recall her debts from those she loved. Despite the desire to lean back into Warrick and close her eyes, she turned to face him, drawing her leg into the seat where it pressed against his. "I can't abandon the people I care about." She didn't have the slightest idea how to stop it, but she couldn't leave Calum to hurt others the way he'd hurt her. Her resolve firmed. "I won't go, even if it costs my life."

Her friends were her life and Inara her home. She could not let either fall to the Trust. It would be impossible to find happiness in another land, with other people, while knowing her own had been left behind and suffered at the hands of the Trust.

She met his eyes. "Tell me how I can help. Tell me how I can stay." *How I can keep Calum from using me against you.*

His gaze roamed over her face as if memorizing it. He was going to make her leave. Giving her up was the only way to salvage any of it.

Any of what, she meant to ask, but his thoughts closed off again. She could only guess at what she saw in his eyes, so green in the light of day. She did not know how it had happened, but she didn't want to leave Warrick, either.

Nim reached forward, running a careful touch over the edge of his brow, a faint thin ridge of scar he must have received as a boy. She had wanted to touch him so badly, though the prospect was much more foolish, since he had every intention of sending her away. Becoming closer would only make it harder, would only make her betrayal hurt worse, because she had no intention of letting him do so. She knew better than to risk what she was about to do.

It didn't stop her.

She leaned forward, closing the distance in painfully slow increments. Warrick could have made her stop. Warrick could have pushed her away.

He didn't. Her lips met his in a soft brush of skin, and his hands came to her waist to draw her nearer. He was warm and yielding and everything Nim hadn't realized she so desperately needed. He held her tightly as she tilted her head to deepen the kiss, warmth flooding through her as his hands slid over her back and hip. She was going to regret kissing him, surely, because she was never going to want to stop.

Her fingers slipped beneath his jacket to run over his chest, edging up again to trail over his neck—drawing him nearer still —then into his soft, dark hair.

Her fingertips brushed the edge of an incongruous spot, short and sharp. Nim froze.

Warrick had made a bargain, like Calum.

Both had a contract somewhere like hers.

She drew away, her eyes slowly opening to find him watching her. *Nim*, he seemed to say. *Nim*. She had the sense that he wanted to reach to stroke her cheek, to tell her that he was sorry, but all she could think of was the lock of hair, so like the one in her own contract. She backed away from him on the chaise to retrieve the crumpled parchment from her tattered jacket, chilled by the loss of his warmth but unable to cease following her concern.

Turning in the seat to read, Nim unrolled the document, its seal broken and spattered with a seneschal's blood. Warrick's blood.

Nim had been a foolish girl, so worried that her father had bargained for beauty, that her face might be scarred. How ridiculous and callow she'd been, wanting to believe it still. She was a pawn, Calum had said, a pawn in a game between heir to the Trust and seneschal of Inara. Her beauty mattered not at all.

Beneath her fingers was a familiar script, the sharp lines of Calum's hand tying her father to a bargain that had cost Nim everything—her family, her freedom, her last bit of hope. She stared at the words for uncountable moments before looking up to stare blankly toward the painting of the slumbering dog.

Nimona's father had not bargained that she might win beauty or a match at court. Nimona's father had reached far higher than anything she could have imagined at all. He'd contracted himself, his family, everything he might ever give. He'd contracted his daughter's future.

Nimona Weston, his only daughter, was to sway the future of all of Inara. She was to decide the fate of its heir.

Behind her, Warrick was silent, his emotions closed off. She felt him move only a breath before his palm pressed against her spine, gentle and warm, his fingertips brushing the bare skin at the base of her neck.

He whispered, "I'm sorry," right before Nimona's world went black.

CHAPTER 29

Nimona awoke in the bed of a wagon, the afternoon sun bearing down on her where she lay on iron slats and weathered boards, a smothering, scratchy wool blanket covering her limbs. Her scar throbbed, and she was jolted as the wagon's wheel hit something. She sat up, head spinning as she squinted to take in her surroundings. Thick forests bordered the field on one side of the wagon, far off mountains to the other. Behind her, two men whose posture seemed suspiciously reminiscent of the castle guard drove a team of horses, and before her, facing the rear of her wagon, was the rutted trail that had led them straight out of Inara.

Nim cursed then stood, tossing off the blanket to curse again. She let loose a string of such vulgar, indecent language that Wesley, sitting in the wagon beside her, stared up at her with an expression that fell somewhere between scandal and awe. The wagon caught on a rut and jostled Nim nearly from her feet. Wesley snatched her leg to steady her, and Nim stared down, furious that she was still in the tattered clothes she'd been wearing when Warrick had incapacitated her with magic.

It appeared that Wesley also wore his same clothes. She flopped down to sitting on the hard planks beside him, taking note of the various bags and supplies riding in indiscriminate piles near the short upright slats. "What did he do, throw us in a wagon the moment I was out?"

Wesley pursed his lips, clearly not eager to tell her.

"For all things sacred, he had the wagon waiting outside the manor the entire time?"

Wesley winced.

Nim groaned and buried her face in her hands. "Will I ever stop being a fool?"

He awkwardly patted her shoulder. "Warrick says that if you learn anything from an experience, then it isn't foolhearted at all."

She raised her face to give him a look. "Too soon, Wes, too soon." He offered her a waterskin, and she took it, drinking greedily despite her anger, which had not fully settled. When she'd had her fill, she leveled her gaze on him again. "Who are these two?"

Wesley cleared his throat, glancing at the men driving the horses briefly before explaining, "The seneschal's personal guard. Trained in weaponry and stealth since they were young, rewarded for chivalry, versed in military…"

His voice trailed off when Nim crossed her arms. "So they're not going to let us talk them into turning around."

He shook his head.

Nim leaned closer. "Wes, you can't truly want to run away. Is there nothing in Inara that you're leaving behind?"

His expression tilted in the strangest manner. When he finally spoke again, his voice was low. "It's my duty, Nim. Not my choice."

For her, Wesley had been thrown out of his home because she was too witless to look out for herself. She turned to the guards. "Stop the wagon." They did not so much as flinch. "Hey!"

"They've been ordered—"

She turned her glare on Wesley, and his words cut off. Nim gauged the distance they'd likely traveled, given that their fight with Calum happened near dawn. It would be too far to walk, should she even be able to outmaneuver two trained guards. She rose to her knees to scrounge through the bags. The scar on her shoulder ached but not more or less when she moved. Nim had feared being marked for so long. She could not regret it—it had saved Alice—but the only other solace she'd felt was that at least it had not been Calum's magic. At least the magic biting her was Warrick's.

She wasn't certain she felt the same once she'd found herself in a wagon outside Inara.

The packs held spare clothes, food, water, and a canvas tent. She slid a clean shirt over her ripped one, deftly maneuvering the tattered material from beneath while Wesley appeared to check the sky for rain. Resuming her rummaging through the largest pack, his eyes returned to her, wary at her intent, she thought, until Nim's hand caught the edge of something heavy, wrapped in several layers of another blanket. She carefully shoved the layers aside to reveal the grip of the fine longsword she'd seen in Warrick's chest of drawers. Nim ran her fingers over the jewel embedded in the pommel.

She glanced back at Wesley, the question clear in her eyes: *Why would he send you a sword when you can't stand to be near it?* More troubling was that Warrick had sent it at all.

Wesley wet his lips. "It's mine."

Nim heard what he didn't say—not from intimations the way she might read from Calum or Warrick but from Wesley's tone, which held years of the same emotion, the torment of speaking of someone who'd done so much wrong.

It wasn't just Wesley's. It had been his father's.

Nim dropped back to land on her bottom with a heavy thump, her eyes going from Wesley to the sword and back again. Wesley's father had a sword fit for a king, laced with magic. She was half certain she was going to be sick.

"Who was he?" she whispered. It was evident the man had not been just Wesley's father, not merely someone who bargained because he was addicted to the draw of magic. He had been someone to the king.

Wesley sighed. "He held office among the court, an advisor to Stewart."

Nim felt herself pale. Wesley, the boy messenger, was more like her than she might have imagined. And Warrick had saved him from the fate Calum had forced upon her.

And Nim's father had bargained so that she alone was to decide the fate of the heir of Inara, a kingdom they'd just left behind.

She swayed. Wesley leaned closer, his bare hand resting over hers. Nim could feel the magic woven through his scars, magic from the Trust.

Warrick had sacrificed himself to save the boy, had broken Nim free of her contract.

"Wes"—she glanced briefly at the backs of the guards—"do you know who Warrick is?"

Wesley's face went a little pale as his scarred fingers curled into the edge of his thin cloak. He did know, and that was clear, but his reply was hedged. "He protected me from the magic of the Trust. I'm bound to him now, and no one else can hurt me with magic."

Nim wasn't certain what she felt safe to admit, but she didn't think Wesley would ever purposefully betray her. Besides, they were on a wagon bound for some far-off land. It wasn't as if it would be easy to steal back into Inara, especially if she'd no idea what the game she'd escaped entailed. "I know who he is," she said. "But the bargain he made with Calum—"

The expression that crossed Wesley's face was complicated, but it was plain it was no small game. Nim lay a hand over Wesley's.

"Rules," he said. "Calum wouldn't stop interfering, so Warrick had to do something, had to set up boundaries to keep him away."

"You know the terms of the contract."

He shook his head. "Only the rules. Calum keeps his magic out of Inara, and Warrick stays above ground, away from the Trust."

And so Calum had decided to use Nim to bypass the rules by sending her where he himself was forbidden. To what end, she didn't know. She might have been meant to send a message, but it seemed that Calum had put much effort into training her well. He must have known, surely, that Nim deciding the fate of the heir of Inara meant the king would eventually succeed in having one.

Unless he'd thought nothing of the sort.

"Wes," she said. "What happens if the king does not have an heir?"

"A council would decide on a new king from among one of the older lines."

"And who"—she swallowed, unable to tolerate the thought —"who would the most likely candidate be?"

Wesley's hand squeezed hers, and Nim closed her eyes. Calum had a man in place who would be king, tied to the magic that was the Trust and under Calum's command.

"But that won't happen, as long as Warrick lives."

Nim's eyes snapped open. She realized, quite suddenly, that Wesley had misunderstood.

Memories of their clash with Calum flashed through her mind. The flames licking shrouded bodies, women who had meant to bring forth a proven heir. The intimations had not been from just Calum. They had come from Warrick as well.

Warrick had been there. Warrick had seen.

Nim recalled the flash of recognition when she'd seen him in the morning light that shone through Hearst Manor, casting away shadows to reveal features she remembered as a girl. Features that had been painted ten feet high through the corridors, features little Nim had thought startling at such a height.

Fates, she'd been obtuse about so many things. The rumors. The stories. It was like cold water thrown in her face.

Nothing about Warrick was unfeeling—he had shown nothing but care. But he had shoved it all away, not because of his brother. He couldn't become attached to anything because it would not be only his downfall. It would be Inara's downfall too.

She remembered the faceoff between Calum and Warrick and Warrick's warning of forfeit if the rules were broken. It seemed very likely that the bargain was all that held a war between magic and the kingdom at bay.

Because Warrick was not just Calum's brother. Warrick was the son of a king. Calum was older and heir to the Trust, but he had no claim to Inara. That was Warrick and Warrick alone.

Nim opened her eyes, giving her gaze to the boy who had just given her the key. Warrick had been trying to buy time with his bargains and allow Calum to believe he was playing the game. But he had sent the prize in a wagon, away from the gameboard, a woman he'd thought was only a pawn.

But Nim held his fate by a deal that had been struck by her father, a deal he'd made with the head of the Trust—the very woman who had borne a king's son and who had prevented that king from having any other heirs. The head of the Trust had sons on opposing sides, and Calum intended to claim both.

"Wesley," she said. "What happens between them now?"

He took a slow breath. "I think Warrick plans to attempt to remove Calum from power himself."

CHAPTER 30

Nim rode in silence for maybe half an hour before her thoughts began to shift into a plan. If Warrick truly believed he could win against Calum, he would have done so already. There was no reason to wait.

There must have been a binding on him from the bargain, some footing he'd lost when he'd set boundaries in his attempt to stave off war.

She'd placed so much blame on fate for her entire life, but it had become clear that she was a fool—nothing of the sort had changed her plans. It had been her father and the Trust. It had been Calum, who had stolen her blood and forced her into the contract because he had known.

Nim wasn't a slave to her fate. She had been wrong all along. Her father had bargained with the head of the Trust, and into the world she'd been born, but not to be a pawn in their game or for some deal that hadn't yet been struck. She had been brushed by the magic of her father's bargain, drawn to it since she was a girl.

Her fate had not been chosen for her. Nim was to be a chooser of fates.

She would not let Warrick die and Inara crumble for some

foolish game. "Wes," she said. "What if you could live out your life as a man far from Inara, never returning?"

He was silent for a long moment, though when he spoke, it seemed as if he'd weighed the answer before. "I wouldn't like that at all, my lady. Inara is my home." *Warrick, too,* she thought, *and duty and honor and the castle he'd roamed as a boy.* They were the same, deep down, only Wes was tied to duty where she was not. Nim was free.

Nothing bound her any longer.

She nodded, resolved to bad decisions and reckless acts as a half-baked plan brought her to her feet.

She drew her fingers from Wes's and stood in one fluid motion, reaching into the bag to grip the solid hilt of a longsword forged by magic. Nim had never used a sword—her weapons were short and light. But clumsy as it was, her swing arced through the air to strike a solid blow to the first guard, slamming into the side of his chest plate and sending him from his seat. She winced as he scrambled for purchase on the side of the wagon, but the horses kept on at speed.

Wasting no time to watch, Nim held the blade to the throat of the second guard, the magic thrumming through her fingers, up her arms, and into her chest. Power sang through her, terrible and exhilarating, but she had no time to dwell on what she was doing or how crazed it might appear. "Stop the horses, or I remove your head."

The guard did draw the animals to a stop—not because he was afraid of her, she was certain, but because he would need to gather his brother in arms and bind Nim in rope to keep her under control.

But when his gaze slid to the weapon leaned against him, his eyes narrowing and his mouth turned down, it was clear he understood. He might easily have bested the woman, but it was not a sword to be trifled with.

Nim was done playing by rules set by her circumstance. She had access to something beyond, something she'd been afraid of since her father had been taken, since she'd first understood it could be used for hurt. But all along, it had not been the thing which was causing her pain.

That had not been the magic. That had been Calum.

Wesley's sword glinted in the late-day sun. It had not drawn her because it was finely made, bedecked with carvings and jewels. The sword had drawn Nim because of its power, and she'd been touched by magic. She could touch it back.

Whatever else the sword was as a weapon, the power that bound it would give her strikes precisely what they needed to allow Nim to escape two king's men. Wesley was to be a great swordsman when he wielded it, but his own father's bargain had cost him the ability to tolerate a blade.

Nim had no such difficulty.

The guard that had been knocked from the wagon had caught up, moving stealthily over the ground behind them, but Nim would waste no time fighting a battle she would most certainly lose. "I'm sorry to do this, but I've no other choice. Take another step, and I will use this sword to run through not just your friend but the boy."

Wes made a sound of disbelief, his wide eyes going from the sword to Nim. "Did you just"—he pressed a hand to his chest —"how?"

"We don't have time for this. Unhitch the horses," she told him. "Now."

Wesley hesitated—surely, Nim thought, considering whether he could take her down, whether he wanted to try. But Nim had the sword, and she would win, and though he had orders, she knew, too, that Wesley did not want to leave his home. Warrick might have been the only father the boy had known. Warrick had kept him safe.

And fates save them both, because Nim was going to risk all of it.

Wesley slid a glance to the guards then did as Nim said. He

was fast, drawing the horses toward the wagon and facing Inara exactly in the manner she would have asked of him.

"I'm sorry," she said again to the guards then gestured to Wes and a horse. "Up," she told him before taking a solid swing at the guard beneath the sword, deliberately striking his armor to avoid badly wounding him but still knocking him well from the seat with the breath from his lungs.

Nim leapt from the wagon and onto a horse, her momentum nearly throwing her over the other side, but Wesley steadied her, and as the second guard made a leaping attempt at them, the boy whipped Nim's horse into a startled gallop with his own mount close behind.

Back to Inara.

CHAPTER 31

T he sun was low in the sky as they neared the border of Inara, but bright fires were lit within the city. Nim slowed her horse, glancing at Wesley. He'd kept pace beside her the entire ride, his competence on horseback evident. "How long before they catch us?" Nim asked.

Wesley didn't glance back to check for the guards, his eyes on the orange glow in the dying light. "Not long. They're two of the most skilled Warrick has. They only let you go because of the sword."

His eyes did not stray to where the weapon rode, shoved between strap and saddle on Nim's mount. "I'm sorry," she told him. "I can't—I couldn't sit by and do nothing."

Wesley's horse tossed its head, but Wes was still. He looked at her, and in his expression was something Nim could not quite make out.

A strange sound echoed from beyond the walls, so Nim did not take the time to ask what had his contemplation. "Can we get back in?"

He shook his head. "Not through the main gate. Warrick will have barred your reentrance." The idea spiked a barb of irritation through her, but Wesley added, "I know a way." He kicked up his horse, riding wide of the walls and toward the line of trees as Nim followed.

They drew up short of the tree line, and Wesley dismounted, drawing to the ground what little tack he'd managed in their haste to escape. "Bring the sword," he told Nim. When she pulled it free and stepped down, he tugged the cinch to release her saddle and sent both animals running with a sharp whistled command. His eyes met Nim's, and they stood for a moment with surely at least one of them considering what a fool thing they were about to do.

"Does Warrick know you can handle the sword?"

Nim frowned. "I hardly think I'd call that handling it. I can use a dagger well enough, but it's not the same sort of beast, is it?" When his expression didn't change, she said, "Oh, you mean touch it? Wes, that's not because of this sword. Your affliction would be toward all swords." Warrick had said he didn't carry his own blade, that he'd left it outside his rooms. The one in Nim's hand had been in his chest of drawers—she'd seen it when he'd caught her, rain-drenched and trying to steal back her things. But surely, Wesley would have understood the boundaries the magic had enacted on him after so much time.

A shout echoed from down the wall, cutting short any further conversation.

Wesley ran into the trees with Nim's other hand in his, dodging past branches and brambles with uncharacteristic ease. It made Nim wonder, strangely, if her first impression had not been awkwardness at all but maybe unease, nervousness at a new introduction. But that made no sense, because as a messenger, Wesley would have been put in such situations on a regular basis. He had been acting peculiar ever since Warrick had told him it was time. Perhaps it was his taking on the responsibility of protecting her or being outside of the castle and away from the eyes constantly upon him. *Or maybe,* Nim thought, *it's the presence of his father's sword.*

"In here," he said, guiding Nim through a narrow opening between the trees.

An uncomfortable sensation rose in her as she followed. Guilt. "Wait," she said, tugging him to a stop. "Maybe you shouldn't go."

He turned to face her where she stood, the sword shoved beneath the belt at her hip, as far away from him as possible. "What do you see?"

It was dim beneath the trees, the shadows barely shifting where they were shielded from the wind by tall stone walls. Nim wasn't certain what she was meant to see, but it wasn't a great deal, aside from Wesley's face. "There's no sense in risking us both. I have to go, Wes, but maybe Warrick was right. Maybe you should leave."

He stared at her for a moment. "You truly have no idea."

"What?"

He took a long breath, ran his free hand over the back of his neck. "For all that is sacred." She started to pull her hand from his, but he only tightened his grip. "Who was your mother, Nim? How long ago did she die?"

A spike of fear shot through her, but not because she was afraid of Wesley, only his questions and secrets she was not meant to speak of. Dark things were meant to stay locked away, deep in that place in her mind. There were things she was not to dwell on no matter what, memories that could make her vulnerable to the magic of the Trust.

"Sixteen years this fall," he told her. "Thereabouts."

Nim's mouth went dry. "How do you know that? You couldn't —you wouldn't even have been born."

"You're right," he said. "My birthday is not until the solstice. In the fall." He stepped closer, wincing at the nearness of the blade. Nim could feel the magic pulse through the scars that threaded his hand. It was hurting him to be so close. He did not step away. "She would have contracted a strange illness," he whispered, "the same as my own mother. Punished for trying to interfere."

Something rent inside Nim. Wes did not sever the connection of their hands.

"My father thought he could fight it with a sword, that a blade could somehow stop what they would do." He was so close that Nim could feel the breath coming out of him, steady and sure, not panicked like hers. "What did *your* father do, my lady? What did he attempt in order to break us all free?"

A muffled shout of king's men on alert echoed through the wall beyond, and Nim became aware that the noises she'd heard had not been simple hanging-day commotion. Something was wrong. It was hanging day, yes, but the king had no men to hang. And Warrick had carted her and Wesley out of the kingdom so he could deal with Calum.

Her gaze shot to Wesley's. "You want to know what my father did." She reached for the crumpled paper that had bound her for so long to the magic of the Trust. "He tied your fate to mine. All of Inara. To me." In the dim light, she let Wesley see the truth in her eyes. "I don't know if you can trust me. I don't know that I'll do what's right." *Or that I'm enough*.

Wes's hand tightened in hers, but he did not take hold of the contract. "You will do what's right. That much I know." What he didn't say lingered in the silence, because neither could know if what was right would be enough to see them through. "You can wield magic that was not bought for you, Nim. What else? Can you see what's coming?"

She shook her head mutely. That was not what deciding meant. She'd no clue at all what was coming.

Wesley held steady. "I've known since I was a boy that my fate would be tied to someone else, that we would all rely on a single hope. I'm glad it's you, Nim. Do what you must."

His trust felt like a kick in the gut. She didn't deserve it. She'd been wrong too many times before. But something tugged at Nim, drawing her toward Inara as if an anchor through her middle, far enough away that she still had her senses but strong enough that it could be nothing but bad. Her gaze fell to the darkness that would lead them past the barriers, distant noises sounding more discontent than before. "I have an unfortunate notion that Calum and Warrick are together, somewhere beyond that wall."

Wesley moved to slide his hand from hers, but she stopped him, unstrapping the small carved mace from her leg. She placed it in his palm. "Follow through with your strikes. Fingers and knees will slow someone down without killing them."

He nodded, taking the weapon as he turned to show her the way through.

Inara was apparently lousy with secret passages, because before Nim could even decide where they might come out, Wesley had slipped through the shadows by a myriad of corridors and hidden entrances, some secreted by magic and some just plain secret.

The pull became more intense, and as they came out of a darkened passage between two tall stone buildings, Nim stumbled, nearly dropping the sword.

She wasn't certain when she'd drawn it from her belt. Wesley stopped, turning to face her. Nim shook her head, the magic tingling through the grip of the weapon making her feel too unsettled to think. "What am I going to do?" she finally asked. "I can't even... I don't know where to start." She would get nowhere in a battle with Calum. She wasn't strong enough, and he had magic. He and Warrick were two of the most powerful men in the kingdom. She had no chance to stand against Calum, no idea how to best someone in a game she wasn't even playing.

"What do you do when you don't know what to do?" she said to the air around her, which was filled with the tingle and sting of magic, the draw she'd been unable to deny.

Wesley moved closer despite his clear revulsion toward the sword. His voice was low, his tone earnest. "I go to Warrick. He's been there for me since I was a boy."

Nim frowned. Obviously, they couldn't do that—he'd just thrown them out of the kingdom. He was likely to lock them in a cell to keep them out of harm's way until he acted out his ill-fated plan. He'd probably already heard they'd returned and had sicced the king's guard on them.

"What do you do?" Wesley asked.

She glanced up at him, emotion clawing its way up her throat. "I go to Margery." Margery was so skilled in contracts and documents that she was sought after at court. Margery knew the truth. "Wesley," Nim said, shoving the sword back into her belt. "I think I have an idea."

CHAPTER 32

Nim had been half afraid to go to Margery, because it would take too long and because Warrick had the manor under watch. But she could feel the draw of magic so strongly and knew that Calum and Warrick were nearly together, somewhere close to the square. Calum would have been stoking the unrest at the lack of hanging while Warrick prepared to implement his plan.

Nim and Wesley rushed down alleyways and passages, the two disturbingly knowledgeable in means of stealth. Wes led her around the manor, through an old servant's entrance, and into a dark hall. When they came through the next corridor, they nearly ran into a startled cousin, Beasley, his hair askew and mouth agape. The plate he'd been carrying crashed to the floor at the sight of Nim scurrying through his family home in the night, wearing pants and with a man in king's colors.

"Margery," Nim demanded.

Beasley gestured vaguely over his shoulder, and Nim gave him a steadying pat on their way past. She and Wesley ran into the study, nearly tumbling in headlong as a maid unexpectedly swung open the door, tea tray in hand. The girl opened her mouth then swung her gaze to Margery.

Margery stood, gesturing the girl away. "Finally," she said. "It's about time you've used some sense."

A SHORT TIME LATER, her head swimming with legal terms and the emotion behind Margery's farewell hug, Nim stood with Wesley at the edge of a crowded square, searching the throng for men of the Trust and men of the king's. Shouts rose through the night air, too warm and too close, and it was evident even to Nim that the king's guard should already have cleared the square. Warrick must have been planning to use the scene as a distraction or some other ploy—she hoped, anyway, because she did not want to think that some other reason was preventing him from enacting order.

Wes sidled closer to the side opposite the sword. He brushed her arm as he drew a small vial from his pocket then handed it to her. "I nearly forgot. From Allister."

Her gaze ran over the hazy liquid within the colored glass.

"He said it would help should you be near overwhelming magic." Wes gestured toward the square, at what would absolutely be an overwhelming task.

"Thank you," she told him, removing the stopper and downing it with an involuntary gag. She shook her head sharply, tucked the empty vial into her pocket, then looked Wesley straight in the eyes. "Are you ready?"

"I don't suppose it matters," he said with a half smile.

She nodded. "I don't suppose it does."

A STRANGE WIND PICKED UP, sharp and sudden, tugging at Nim's hair and snapping the banners overhead. She followed the draw through the square, the thick crowd of wide skirts and sword-wielding revelers parting for her despite seeming unaware they'd done so. The air smelled of sweat and ale, of greasy meat and backstreet taverns. It was not the courtiers about but the citizens who were most at risk from dealings with the Trust.

Wesley followed cautiously at her side, his fingers wrapped around the mace. Nim did not know whether it was Allister's tonic or the stinging bite of the magic through the sword, but she had not yet fallen prey to the loss of sensation she usually felt.

Calum's power was calling her, drawing her in despite that he had no contract binding her. It was not that he owned her any longer but something more—the magic of the Trust.

He wanted her there with him. To hurt Warrick.

She choked back any notion of sentiment, forcing her steps forward. No matter how well her plan played out, it was going to hurt more than a little.

Nim stepped from the throng of revelers into a wide, open circle at the center of the square. The citizens of Inara carried on around them as if entirely unaware they'd left the space, as if two dangerous men had not squared off in the public courtyard before them.

Warrick's sword was drawn, Calum's cane in hand. Nim had the sense the two were waiting, for their agreement meant that one must not act until the other had broken the accord and its laws.

She was not certain which man the intimations came from as she stepped forward, but she did sense when Warrick realized she was there. His jaw went tight, his shoulders shifting into a more ready stance. Heat rose through the square, the wind whipping at her from two directions. Wesley's cloak brushed against her, his eyes on Warrick, a reminder that Nim could not fail. She wasn't risking just herself.

She took a steadying breath then strode forward, Warrick's magic pressing against her, urging her to stop. But Calum's power fought with her, because it could only benefit him if she was near—a distraction to his opponent.

Power writhed around her booted feet, wrapping her calves

as she crossed the stone that lined the square. It hissed and popped near the blade of the sword, sending stinging bites through her hand and crackling through the very air she breathed. She kept on.

Warrick snapped a command at his guard, and two men jerked alert, seemingly surprised to find the strange scene of their seneschal facing off with the heir to the Trust. They rushed toward Nim, but Wesley was faster. He cut them off, mace in hand, and ordered both to stop. Warrick's disbelief swam over Nim, but she didn't have time to process it before his anger rose anew. He was practically shouting at her to get away, but he might as well have said so aloud given the expression on Calum's face.

Calum's posture had gone lazy, his cane draped over a shoulder as Nim strode toward him, his smile wicked and gleaming in a gloat that he had won some special prize. It was no task to keep her expression plain with dread, because Nim had no deuced idea if what she meant to do would even work.

"Lady Nimona," Calum purred. "What a pleasure that you have joined us." His mouth quirked in its grin. "And what a lovely sword." He let his gaze drift to Warrick. "Though, I confess, I did think you preferred a dagger. Something close, easily in hand."

Warrick's fury was a fire inside her, but Nim did not look his way. She could not take her eyes off of Calum, not when he could strike at any moment, faster than a snake and twice as venomous.

"I come to propose a bargain," she said.

Calum's shoulders shook in a laugh. His cane swung to the ground, the tip touching stone as he leaned forward, his long jacket draping toward his bare hand. "My lady, I'm honored, truly. But you could have nothing at all I could possibly want."

"My terms," she said, holding the parchment forward in her free hand.

Calum's mouth flinched in something of a tell, but his intimations felt as confident and cruel as ever. "You can stop there," he told her. His gaze narrowed. "Honestly, Nimona, I'm going to enjoy what I'll do to you once this whole thing is done."

Nim swallowed hard. "What are you afraid of, Calum?"

His dark eyes shot to hers. She wasn't certain she'd ever called him by his name to his face. He let her feel that he liked that she was being so unreasonable and brave, as the fight in her would make his game so much more enjoyable.

"Nimona," Warrick barked.

Nim did not look at him, despite what she felt roiling through the square. She hoped Wes reached him in time. She hoped their plan worked. Warrick was forced to keep his distance, he and Calum in a confrontation that was bound by rules. Nim held no such ties. Not any longer.

"Just the two of us," she told Calum. She reached into the loose neck of her shirt and snapped the thin chain free then palmed the ring, its magic pale in comparison to the sword.

Delight swam through Calum, spilling out to touch her in a way that made her skin crawl. She still wasn't certain what a gift freely given meant, but she knew it held power. Warrick had done something in the gesture, something that had either tied her to him or protected her in some small way from his brother.

She tossed the ring to the ground.

Calum laughed, loudly and unreservedly, his hand coming to rest over his chest as he looked at his brother. Warrick's intimation held utter disbelief tinged with horror, but Nim could not spare him a glance. She rushed forward, closing the distance, swinging the sword with everything she had in a low arc that rose toward Calum's chest.

He did not even look at her as his hand effortlessly snatched the blade midair, inches from his form. He was chuckling like a dog with two tails that Nimona had attacked him—he had legal recourse to end her, and Warrick could do nothing to stop it.

Power surged through her palm at her grip on the sword, burning in a manner that did not seem real—it was too painful to fathom. She drew the blade down against Calum's palm, free of his hand, then dropped it. As it fell to the stones with a clatter, Nim straightened, moving forward into Calum's grip. She wasn't certain he realized and wasn't certain whether she meant to or if he had drawn her there, but it was exactly where she needed to be.

She whispered into his ear, her words vile and dark, and his grin slid into something more wicked as his face turned to hers. She was nearly in his embrace, and she felt Warrick rushing them and knew without a doubt he was going to break the terms of his agreement. Calum would win.

"You," she said to Calum, "are going to regret every thought you ever had of me."

His breath brushed over the heated skin of her face. "Lady Nimona, you know I love it when you talk to me in such ways." His free hand came toward her, his intent to wrap it around her neck tortuously plain, just as Wesley slammed into Warrick and just as Nim's hand slid into Calum's open palm, along the cut from the magic blade.

Calum's brow tilted, and then, in a rush, heat spread through Nim's entire being, bringing an agony that was entirely familiar.

He dropped her like she was molten, his roar cutting the air and rattling through the marrow of her bones. She hit the ground hard, gasping for breath, the bloody parchment crushed in her grip.

Warrick was on Calum before the magic had finished its work, their power clashing in a wave of energy that made her retch. She rolled to her stomach, the sword loose beneath her boots, Wesley rushing to help her out of the way.

It was too much power, and Calum couldn't fight it. As soon as the magic took hold, he would be unable to act, bound by the contract in her hands, his freedom stolen the way he'd stolen hers as a girl. Warrick's magic would seal it. Warrick would have control. Wes's hands were on Nim's shoulders, drawing her back, but he was knocked down by a blow of magic, stumbling backward beside her as they both watched the melee in horror. The crowd shifted from their circle as Warrick and Calum rolled over the stones like grappling animals, a wolf and a snake locked in battle, their teeth bared and grips unrelenting.

Calum slammed his brow against Warrick's cheek, snapping his teeth for purchase and digging his clawed fingers into seneschal robes. Warrick's elbow crashed into his brother's jaw, their legs shifting in a wild scramble for a foothold, every muscle tensed. Blood was smeared over Calum's face, and Warrick's expression twisted in pain and rage.

The air crackled with energy that felt like a coming storm, and something far beneath the earth rumbled. They lost the last of their control on the audience, and startled gasps and shouts rose through the square. The king's guard stepped forward, but the men of the Trust only watched.

They, Nim realized, were held to the laws of Inara. Unlike the king's guard, they would know that Warrick was Calum's brother. And they belonged to the true head of the Trust, not Calum. Not yet.

Power slammed into Nim, and she retched again, rolling away from Wesley and the fighting to press herself to the cool stones. She kicked the blade from beneath her feet, though a deep, dark part of her wanted to take hold of it, to grab the stinging hilt, cross the space, and ram it through Calum's chest.

She could not.

It was too late for that.

She had only one chance.

Warrick slammed Calum onto his back across the stones of the square. Calum was bound in irons, his wrists chained before him, blood draining from his mouth and across his brow. His cut palm was clenched into a fist, knuckles white with his rage. He hissed a curse for his brother and the filthy Inaran wench it could only be assumed was Nim, but Nimona did not give the man a second glimpse, because Warrick's gaze rose to hers.

Sprawled over the ground, slicked with sweat and heaving in

gasps of breath, Nim let him have her gaze, as freely as ever. Warrick's eyes were dark as he rose from Calum's form and strode toward her with a fisted hand. He reached for the parchment she'd lost in her writhing pain, bending at the waist before standing over her. His expression was unreadable, his emotions in check, but his gaze flicked to Wesley in something that said they were going to have a talk about things later.

Warrick's strong hands unrolled the parchment smeared in Calum's blood, and as he read the words of a contract written in Margery's hasty hand, one side of his lips tipped up in a furtive smirk. He opened his palm to glance inside, where Wesley had delivered two small emerald gems, as green as Warrick's eyes.

"Guard," Warrick snapped, suddenly the seneschal again. "Take this prisoner to the king."

The crowd's chatter rose, movement resuming throughout the square, and Warrick knelt to pick up the tiny silver band and a magic-forged sword. He stood, the weapon so much smaller in his grip than it had felt in hers, and stared down at Nimona. "Clean these two up," he told the guard, "and deliver them to my rooms."

CHAPTER 33

Nim had been cleaned and sorted, dressed in a simple black gown trimmed with ribbon, its bodice and sleeves slim against her battered form. She was delivered to Warrick's sitting room and parked in a chair opposite Wesley, whose hair was still damp and skin slightly flushed. He did not say a word but eyed her conspiratorially, and though Nim wasn't convinced the two weren't about to be punished, she couldn't say she was disappointed with how things had turned out. Even if she were hanged, Calum was bound by contract.

He could not hurt her ever again.

No fewer than six guards watched them as they sat, and a dozen more waited in the corridor outside. Warrick was with the king, likely sorting the mess that was explaining Calum and deciding how to deal with a lady who'd fallen from good society and a mutinous messenger.

The tapers had burned low when he finally arrived, though the windowless room gave her no indication of how late it truly was. Wesley, settled back into his chair, yawned wide, but his gaze abruptly went sharp. He looked so young, so much a boy. She felt an overwhelming need to protect him.

Warrick charged into the room like a bull, shoulders broad

beneath the robes and jacket of his station, his collar slightly askew. The air punched from Nim's lungs. "Out," he told the guards.

Wes straightened, but Nim had never managed to relax. The seneschal's gaze slid between them, daring either to speak a word. "You're a fool," he told Nim as soon as the door latched behind him. He gestured vaguely through the air toward Wes. "And you followed her into this half-witted plan that could have seen you both killed."

Wesley, fates save him, nodded. Nim pressed her lips together, praying for the boy. Warrick's fisted hands came to his sides, then he tossed his robe angrily to a chair beside Wes.

"You wouldn't have hurt us," Wesley said.

Nim tried to warn him off with a look, but he couldn't be stopped. Apparently, she decided, Wesley could not feel Warrick's intimations, or he would have held his cursed tongue.

"I knew you wouldn't act in any way that might bring her harm and that you would trust us."

Us. Warrick's gaze was hard on Wesley, and Nim felt a shiver of something down the back of her neck.

When he finally spoke, his voice was low. "I might have hurt you by mistake."

"I trust her," Wesley said, "as much as I trust you."

The heat of his anger seemed to ebb, replaced by the terrible ideas of what might have gone wrong, of how close it had come. Nim could not look at them, at the imaginings of exactly how it might have played out. She felt herself sway, the first she'd done in all the hours they'd waited.

"Oh no, you aren't." Warrick's voice was close, his hands on her shoulders, forcing her to look at him.

"We need sleep," Wesley said with a yawn. "We've had none since you tossed us out of Inara."

Warrick's expression went into a hard line, the boy trying patience that had already worn too thin. "Sleep, then," he told Wes, "but this conversation is not done." Wes nodded, sliding back into the chair to draw Warrick's robe over himself as a blanket, and Nim was unceremoniously swept from first her chair and then the room.

Warrick slammed the door to the study behind them, striding across the space in what should have been far too few steps to deposit her in the plush chair near the hearth. The room was cool, lit only by moonlight, the orange glow of morning nowhere in sight. It had felt like years, and yet it was not even dawn.

He shoved a glass of amber liquid into her hands. "I'm afraid you'll have to remain under the king's protection. The Trust will not let this go unanswered."

"The king's protection?" her voice was low and more tremulous than she liked. She stared at the liquid, wondering if she truly wanted to take the edge of numbness off, to face what she'd done. *Protection*.

Warrick crossed his arms. "Mine."

Her gaze traveled up the length of him to land on his striking green eyes. She tossed back the drink, gasping as it seared her throat.

Warrick took the glass from her.

"How would that work, precisely?" As if she had a choice in the matter. She was lucky to be counted among the living.

He knelt before her, his hands only inches from the cambric of her skirt. "You would not be bound to me by magic, Nim. I will not tie you the way you were shackled by terms before. Protection is what I mean, and only that." His eyes fell to her hands where they twisted in her lap, fingers still raw and stinging from the sword. "Hearst Manor belongs to the king now. You may stay there, under guard but free to do as you wish. Allister and Alice are to be custodians of the property. They are henceforth employed by the kingdom and will face no scrutiny for recent events."

Emotion welled up, nearly choking Nim, and she tightened her fingers in knots. Margery was safe. Alice and Allister were safe and would be provided for in ways beyond anything they might have come to expect. Warrick had done that. "What if I say no?"

His eyes snapped from their tracking of the movement of her hands to Nim's face. He didn't want harm to come to her. He wanted to protect her.

"What if I..." She swallowed, forcing herself to say the words, willing any grateful tears from falling. "What if I'd rather stay here?"

The sharp tilt to Warrick's brow melted away, and he came forward to his knees, sliding his hands into hers, untangling the knot of her fingers to rest them in his. "Nim," he said, the word a vow, an oath that spoke of worship, devotion, and something Nim could not focus on because he'd moved even nearer, leaning over her to draw her forward, cradling her before him so that his breath trailed over the bared flesh of her neck and face.

"If you stayed here, I would be forced to treat you as you deserve." There was a delicious uncertainty to the word that skittered over Nim's flesh, but Warrick's reply broke off as he paused to lean in and brush his lips softly over the curve of her jaw. His promises were a whisper against her flesh. "I would be forced to elevate you above court, to give you a title that warranted the respect of your station"—his nose grazed her neck, down and back as his mouth rose painfully near her lips —"of my partner." *My equal.*

Nim's breath deserted her.

He seemed to recognize the question in her gaze. "Partner," he repeated as he came forward again, his gaze skimming down briefly to her skirts. His voice held a growl of approval. "An occupation in which you're free to wear pants." His eyes met hers again, his lips coming finally against her own. Warmth rushed through Nim, so strong that she nearly did not notice the press of his hand in hers. She drew away from his kiss, and he raised her hand between them, to the thin band of metal that rested on her finger, the ring she'd tossed to the ground.

"Protection?" she asked.

Warrick's smile was devastating. "Just a ring, though I'm not certain we can get the king's approval to skip the contract." His expression shifted. "It was your mother's. She gave it so that you might be safe."

Something strange fluttered through Nim, something she wasn't sure she'd felt before. It was not terribly uncomfortable. "A long engagement?"

Warrick sent her an intimation of his closed bedroom door, the two of them behind it in the dark, and Warrick holding her against him as the sun rose in the room beyond. "Not very, if I can help it."

The fluttering in Nim broke into a sensation that rose through her, bursting free in a quiet, breathy laugh. And then she had hold of him by the tie of his shirt, drawing her to him for a deeper, lingering kiss. "I agree to your terms."

EPILOGUE

W arrick strode into the king's private study as seneschal
of Inara, as a man summoned. Because despite everything else, Warrick was somehow still both of those things.

The king glanced up at him and shooed an attendant away.
The king did not offer Warrick a seat, only flicked his chin in
another impatient gesture, one to draw him near.

"Your Majesty," Warrick said, dipping into a bow before the
man's chair. Stewart grew paler every year, his blond hair fading
to silver and his beard so long he'd started wearing it in braids. It
pained Warrick to see him age, and not simply because he would
miss the father who'd raised him.

The king harrumphed. "Stand up. No one's here to see you."

Warrick gave him a sideways glance. They both knew it was
no social visit. Warrick had risen at the sting of unfamiliar
magic, which drew him from his bed far too soon, certain that
he would be called to the source.

The head of the Trust might have sent anyone at all into the
castle without the use of magic. She had wanted him to sense it,
to understand what she was about.

Warrick had known it would not take long for her to respond
or for his mother to discover that Warrick had captured his

brother and held him bound beneath the castle. It was not only that she would have Calum back. She wanted more.

Calum was heir to the Trust, but the queen would not be satisfied until she held both the undercity and Inara. And Warrick was the son of a king.

One kingdom had never been enough for her. Warrick didn't see why she would stop at two.

Before him, Stewart ran a hand over his beard, the rings heavy and askew on crooked fingers that had not healed properly after a long-ago break. "She taunts me," he said, "even now."

Warrick stood silently. There was no comfort to offer, not from him. He did not relish seeing his father's torment, but nothing would bring him to say, "There's still time. You could produce another heir." Not when he'd watched so many women come into the castle only to be burned beneath their shrouds.

Not when he could still see the flames licking over their forms, devouring, decimating, a tithe to the toll of the magic.

Stewart drew a slow breath then gestured to a letter that rested on the center of his desk. Warrick realized that it had been left untouched. The king had found it on his desk in the center of his private study, a place that was guarded and warded and should have remained safe.

His dark eyes came to Warrick's. "We've not much time, do we, you and I?"

She's coming for us, the words seemed to imply, but no one could read the thoughts of the king. Stewart prided himself on being an unpredictable man. That kept his people—and his enemies—guessing.

Warrick moved to the desk and picked up a message that had been intended for both him and his father. The parchment was vellum, folded and tucked into an envelope, unaddressed and unsealed but tingling with potent magic.

When Warrick opened it, a thin chain fell out, and on it, a silver ring.

His chest gave a painful squeeze, followed swiftly by the

sharp sting of anger and something more possessive and protective than was entirely safe. But it was not the one he'd given Nim, only a duplicate. Warrick understood the warning as plain as the day. His father had been right. The Trust was coming for them all.

Warrick stepped closer to kneel before his father. "I'll stand with you," he vowed, "as I always have."

Stewart leaned forward to grip Warrick's shoulder, his hand still strong despite that he was more than twice Warrick's age. "You'll stand with Inara," he answered, "even as she tries to burn our kingdom to the ground."

THE STORY CONTINUES

Please look for *Between Ink and Shadows* book two: *Before Crown and Kingdom*

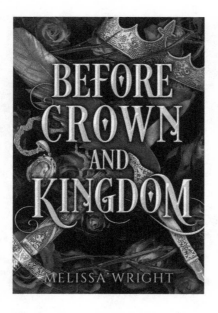

Freedom was more treacherous than she ever imagined.

Nimona Weston's debts are paid. Her contract with the dark society known as the Trust is broken. But the magical ties that bind her to a long-ago bargain are rooted deep.

She's thrust back into the life she'd been forced from as a girl and now her every move is under the watchful eye of the king. A king who wants her dead. But fate has plans of its own and Nim is helpless to stop them, even as the future of the kingdom is placed in her hands.

Find it now at your favorite retailer.

ALSO BY MELISSA WRIGHT

- STANDALONE FANTASY -

Seven Ways to Kill a King

- SERIES -

BETWEEN INK AND SHADOWS

Between Ink and Shadows

Before Crown and Kingdom

THE FREY SAGA

Frey

Pieces of Eight

Molly (a short story)

Rise of the Seven

Venom and Steel

Shadow and Stone

Feather and Bone

DESCENDANTS SERIES

Bound by Prophecy

Shifting Fate

Reign of Shadows

SHATTERED REALMS

King of Ash and Bone

Queen of Iron and Blood

- WITCHY PNR -

HAVENWOOD FALLS

Toil and Trouble

BAD MEDICINE

Blood & Brute & Ginger Root

❧

Visit the author on the web at

www.melissa-wright.com